WHAT READERS SAY ABOUT ROBERT'S BOOKS

Move over Elmore

"Love the dialogue and the character studies...definitely a blend of Mickey Spillane and Elmore Leonard."
~ Amazon reviewer Alex Adamson

"You're guaranteed a mighty fine read." ~ Claude Bouchard, author of *The Vigilante Series*

"Robert Chazz Chute is such a skilled spinner of tales that the reader is more than willing to suspend any possible disbelief to go along for the ride." —David Pandolfe, author of *Jump When Ready*

"It's not very often one finds a writer with such a dark side that has such a great sense of humor." —Glenn Roberts, Amazon reviewer

"Robert Chazz Chute proves that genre fiction can be inventive and unconventional in its use of language while delivering a suspenseful story."
~ Dream Beast, Amazon reviewer

An Excellent Read

"I loved this book. It is well written, fast paced and unusual for a gangster book."
~ M Slott, Amazon reviewer

Bigger Indeed!

"Oh wow. What can I say? Mr. Chute pulled me in with his POV and kept the twists coming through the whole book.

I found the ending to be delightful and perfect. With comedy throughout and a wonderful cast of characters."

~ Jo Michaels, Amazon reviewer and author of *The Fury*

Excellent, fast paced romp

"This book plays out like a Guy Ritchie film. The pacing is frenzied, the plot convoluted yet easy to parse, and the characters larger than life. Half the fun is trying to who's trying to betray who. I would whole-heartedly recommend this novel to action fans and can't wait to grab the author's next work in this series."

~Amazon reviewer Rev357

What a fun ride of a crime thriller!

"In a short span of a couple of short stories collections and a few novelettes, Robert Chazz Chute has seriously become one of my favourite authors! You can count on him for well-written stories that pack punch, plot twists, clever dialogue and even some hidden wisdom in their pages."

~ Amazon reviewer johligo

Five Stars

"Great treat, fun, unpredictable and gritty." ~ Kindle customer, Amazon reviewer

"Suspense, humor, love!" ~ Shirleyjack, Amazon reviewer

"Genuine characters, full of ups and downs. Intricate plot." ~ Julio Wickham, Amazon reviewer

Good Thriller

"Kept my attention. Real page turner could not stop reading till I finished the entire book. Read it in one day." ~ Amazon reviewer A. Alpuche

5.0 out of 5 stars Do Not Miss This Book!

"Chazz is the master. Every story he writes immerses you so deeply in its world, you can barely crawl out when the pages are closed."

~ Amazon review by Alex Kimmell, author of *The Key to Everything*

"The author has a definite talent with words and ideas." —Love to Read!, Amazon reviewer

"His words lift and dance off the page, bringing the story to life." —Kindle Customer, Amazon reviewer

"The world building is horrifically well done with twists and turns and deceit around every corner." —Wanda, Amazon reviewer

"Nothing but sheer exhaustion could tear my eyes from the captivating dance of words choreographed by Robert Chazz Chute." —Halph Staph, Amazon reviewer

"Wonderful action constantly holds your interest." —Sharon Finn, Amazon reviewer

RESURRECTION

A HIT MAN THRILLER

ROBERT CHAZZ CHUTE

Resurrection
A Hitman Thriller
Robert Chazz Chute

Published by Ex Parte Press

ISBN (paperback): 978-1-927607-56-5

ISBN (ebook): 978-1-927607-57-2

This book is a work of fiction. Any references to historical events, real people, or real places are used fictitiously. Other names, characters, places, and events are products of the author's imagination, and any resemblance to actual events, or places, or persons, living or dead, is entirely coincidental.

DEDICATION

Special thanks to Gari Strawn of strawnediting.com and to Russ Sawatsky for their invaluable editorial assistance. I appreciate all they do for me. Another big thank you goes to J, C & C without whom none of my work would be possible.

CONTENTS

FOREWORD

About *Resurrection*

If this is your first encounter with the *Hit Man Series*, welcome and thanks for jumping in! For all those who wanted more Jesus in their lives, welcome back to the world of the divine assassin. You don't have to start with *Bigger Than Jesus* and work your way up to *Resurrection*. Though this is technically the fourth book in the *Hit Man Series*, you can enjoy each book as a stand-alone and not miss a beat.

I decided to build out the *Hit Man Series* because of requests from readers. Fans of the first three books will note that Jesus Diaz does not show up on the first page of *Resurrection*. He does appear soon enough and the action cranks along nicely.

The roots of this story reach back to when we first met Jesus hanging off the ledge of a tall building on a rainy night in New York. Jesus has grown since then. He's talking to himself less and trying to overcome the demons of his terrible past. Our anti-hero's point of view has changed and the storytelling is more conventional. I hope to reach new readers with *Resurrection* and still hold on to the fans who fell in love with Mr. Diaz in New York. No matter where you drop into his missions, I hope you have a good time.

Readers who enjoy the *Hit Man Series* will find there's some crossover with *The Night Man*, another crime series I began recently. If you enjoy Jesus Diaz, you're going to love Easy Jack in *The Night Man*. There will be more crossovers in future books. Jesus teams up with Easy in the next book of the *Night Man Series*. It's called *In Dark Hours*.

Wherever my words find you, I hope you are free or close to something like it.

Happy reading!

~ RCC

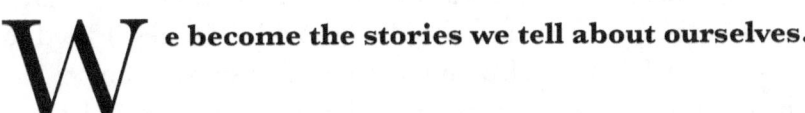

We become the stories we tell about ourselves.

Like you, I want a lot of things. I want rich, dark coffee every morning, two cream, one sweetener. I don't want to have to be anywhere in particular by nine o'clock. I would prefer warm breezes and a fine house on a tropical beach. Some think I want too much. On the night in question, my chief desire was to avoid getting shot.

While normal folks hustled to their jobs, appointments and errands, I used to do touristy things in London. I lingered in cafes and read novels without paying attention to the time, no schedule or routine. I had a cozy out-of-the-way flat and I'd built a gaming computer. My only furniture was a bed, a gaming chair, a desk for the computer's two screens and an easel in the corner by the window.

Games on Steam and Twitch would have to wait. Trouble had found me. In my case, Trouble was the corpse slumped in my gaming chair and, to stay alive, I had to make more people into corpses.

I'd been avoiding trouble quite well by staying on the move for the last couple of years. Sun-drenched Spain was warmth and happiness. Smiles and laughter seemed to come to the Spanish more easily. Though I have Spanish blood, New York beat that capacity for easy smiles out of me. I kept going, losing myself *in* crowds but never managing to lose myself *to* crowds.

I thought Italy would be my home for a while. Rome is a castle that contains all the history and art we want to remember.

Though I loved the city, my mother didn't feel I was safe there. "At the Vatican, you are too close to God and He is always watching," she told me. "People like us are meant for the Colosseum, maybe, but not for churches full of old men praying hard because they're too scared of dying."

So I kept moving.

Echoes of ancient Rome haunt London's architecture. I enjoyed the friendly energy in the pubs as I sipped dark beer. I drank in arch British accents spoken in hushed tones in old bookstores. I liked to people-watch while I traveled on the Tube. The smooth tone of the recorded voice that warned me to "mind the gap" cheered me. I loved London's sights, especially the Sherlock Holmes statue at Baker Street Station and Madame Tussauds wax museum.

The freaky torture chamber in the wax museum was good mental preparation for the horrors ahead. I didn't know it then but my history had set me on one path to the future. No more detours or carefree afternoons in cafés.

Losing oneself had been such comfort but Camberley is a small city of about 38,000. I stepped off the train in Camberley and paused to get my bearings. I envied the other passengers returning home late from work. Their day was at an end. The night shift was just beginning for me.

I was only a couple of hours from my home in London but I felt exposed. This was the kind of place that was small enough for people to make eye contact. A small population invites familiarity, observation and casual conversation. Those are dangerous behaviors for someone like me. I was born for the underworld.

The sky brightened at random intervals as sporadic fireworks burst over Camberley. *Guy Fawkes Day.* "Gunpowder, treason and plot," I said aloud to no one. My life in New York used to be about those three things. Despite my best efforts, I was about to return to that life. I should have gotten back on the train. I should have taken those fireworks as an omen and run.

The Guy Fawkes celebration was not that big a deal in Camberley. I regretted missing the light show over Parliament. However, history is indelible. It asserts itself in a way that the unknown future cannot. Ghosts from my old life had traveled all the way from New York to haunt me. I didn't use my New York name anymore but somehow they tracked me down.

When I crossed the ocean to escape New York, I left dead men in my wake. It was fight or flight. To escape, I had to do a little of both. NYC had come to Camberley and it would be — *had to be—* bloody. There was no other way. I wished I was walking with Jesus. Jesus Diaz would understand my plight.

The wind picked up as I wandered away from the train station, wary of CCTV. That was London's one negative for people like me: too many surveillance cameras.

The first cabbie I found had a Cockney accent so thick I could barely understand him. He spoke loudly, shout-talking as if the back seat of the cab was the back of a theater. He turned in his seat to talk to me often, his gaze felt like mice crawling over my chest.

"Take me here," I said, and held out a scrap of paper. The address was a scrawl that was not my own. I scratched out some numbers and added a few to put some distance between me and the target. I would be close but the cab wouldn't drop me off in front of a future crime scene, either.

The cabbie turned on the dome light to peer at the address again as if he was deciphering a complex code. Before he was done, he turned to take another long look at me.

I'm used to creepy stares from ogling men. I try to take lust as a compliment if guys aren't too piggy about it. As long as their rudeness doesn't get in my way or hold me back, I ignore them.

However, that night I was in a hurry. "Hey! Can you get me there or not? If not, let me know now and I'll grab another cab. I'm not here so you could gawk at my tits."

He shrugged, turned off the dome light and went about his business, embarrassed. I'd come off too strong, not because I called him out but because I didn't want to be memorable. When I lived in New York, I had to be aggressive all the time. It's how you make your way through the city. Push, or you're a pushover.

The cab rolled to a stop in front of an old, narrow house. No light shone from the building's windows. I grabbed my duffel bag and climbed out. I tossed the cabbie his fare with a couple of pounds for a tip.

He waited to watch me go into the house. Maybe he was thinking of my safety or perhaps he was staring at my ass in his headlights. I headed toward a small shop, the only source of light on the street. By the time I came back out with a pack of cigarettes and a Coke, the cab had disappeared.

Up the hill, the silhouettes of iron gates stood tall against the city shine. I walked that way and, on the stone wall by the gate, spotted the numbers I was looking for.

I wanted to go back to my flat in Muswell Hill. After a calming hour or two of playing *GTA 5* or *Fortnite* or *Black Ops 4*, I might relax. But there was still the problem of the dead woman in my gaming chair. I didn't know how I was going to get rid of the body yet.

To calm myself, I could have tried my hand at copying Salvador Dali's style of painting. Getting the colors right is relatively easy, but to imitate the master's brush strokes is like forging another person's handwriting. Dali's work was chock-full of surreal images. I love surreality because, too often, reality sucks.

But I had to face reality. My father was Pete Vasquez, a captain for New York's Spanish mob. Dad started out as an enforcer and graduated to bookie, sometimes a shylock. I knew he was a made guy early on but he admitted nothing about his membership in the Machine for a very long time.

It was my mother who trained me to run *at* problems, not *from* them. Like the Devil, I have used many aliases. My real name is Lily Olivia Vasquez. I am a target but I will not be a victim anymore.

The buzzer at the front gate had no cameras that I could see. I tossed the duffel over the fence and climbed the stone wall. I do a lot of Pilates. I'm up to it. I managed to avoid rolling my ankle when I dropped to the other side. The easy part was over.

The ground was soft from the day's rain so I left a footprint behind me with every step. Since I'm not a ninja, I didn't know what I could do about that. My policy is I don't dwell on things I can't control.

I'd come for men trying to track, control and kill me. I had heavy experience dealing with men who tried to tell me what to do, to dominate and own me. They were all history. If they were not forgotten, they soon would be.

I stuck to the tree line and ducked behind a hedge where the trees thinned. A light popped on. Two men were speaking in weirdly aggressive tones. They spoke in that tone men use when the subject is sports and each is loyal to rival sports teams. Breakin' balls, in other words.

As I crept closer I discovered their accents were American. Specifically, this pair was brought up in Brooklyn. They were so careless and loud, they couldn't have suspected they were being observed. Unless I'd stumbled upon a mansion that's a halfway house for hearing-impaired bad guys, these big dopes must have been at least a little drunk.

The light went out again as I heard a door close. The two men remained, smoking and relaxed, far too lackadaisical have been on guard duty. They weren't expecting trouble. They probably assumed I was dead. That was good. My death was an integral part of my plan.

Both men — one tall and skinny, the other short and round — looked startled as I stepped out from behind the hedge not ten feet away. They turned and stared. Maybe it was the booze or perhaps they'd always had brains that worked arduously, as if they were mired in deep mud.

"Hey, Red!" the tall one called out.

I tossed my hair and beamed a smile. The red locks were new. I'd bought the wig in Kensington. People would remember the bright red hair. They were less likely to remember my face. One defining feature blurred the other details. After that night, I couldn't pretend to be a redhead again, not on this continent, anyway.

The tall one smiled at me with a mouthful of teeth that seem to wander across his wide mouth aimlessly. "Ooh, what's your name?"

"Cherry's the name, boys." My English accent wasn't bad. My voice was steady as I tested it on them. If I failed the accent test, the evening would end prematurely and badly. I liked my new black leather jacket. I didn't want to see it turned into a sieve with my blood leaking through.

Both men looked me over. It was an appraising look, different from those of flirts and oglers. They knew the name Cherry. They were deciding how nervous they should be around me.

Pulling off a scam requires confidence. I'd always had my share of that. My mother taught me how to swagger the same week I got my first period. "Walk like you're somebody who is going to own the world," she told me, "because you are."

She had me walk back and forth across the room. "No, not like a dude with your shoulders up. Move like a panther. A woman who owns herself moves like a panther."

I'd seen one panther asleep at the Bronx Zoo. Still, I knew what she meant. I tried my stride again and Mama gave me a slight nod that I took for grudging approval. I almost had it, but obviously, I didn't have it quite right.

"How will I know for sure when I've got it?" I asked.

"You'll know when you walk like me," Mama said.

The short one wasn't as friendly as his fellow guard. "You lost? You might be lost, pretty lady."

"She said she was Cherry," the tall one said.

"I heard what she said," the short one replied, "but we have to be sure. You're on private property, Miss … uh — "

"Cherry. I was on a job for your boss and — "

"What kind of job?"

The short one thought he was a big guy but he was just a fat guy. As he slipped from curiosity to a lascivious stare, I decided to kill him first.

"Take it easy, Short Round," I said. "It was a collection job." I slipped the duffel from my shoulder, pulled it open and flashed the cash, lots of it. Money was the calling card that opened doors everywhere.

Short Round peered in. "Now, how'd you get all that?"

"Sold a lot of Girl Scout cookies. What do you think?"

"Have you still got your Girl Scout uniform?" the tall one asked.

I liked him even less then. "I retrieved the money and killed the bitch. Your boss will want the dough, am I right?" My New York accent slipped in a little just then but the guards' gaze was fixed on the duffel.

"Arms up. We'll have to frisk you." The tall one said it but they both stepped closer.

"Both of you?"

"Thoroughly."

I decided I didn't like the tall one any better than the short one.

"Where you from, girl?" Short Round asked.

When I'm in situations like this, I always ask myself the same question: What would Jesus do? Jesus Diaz was good at talking himself out of tight spots. I should do that. However, when Short Round came at me with his big hands, palms out and aiming for a free grope, I decided to be myself instead. I dropped my attempt at an English accent. "I'm the woman you meet at the place where your dreams and nightmares meet."

Short Round looked at me like a terrier confused by an escalator. I pulled my handgun out of the bag and shot him in the face. Predictably, one shot did the job. Short Round crumpled to the ground.

I lined up my next shot. The tall one was pulling a pistol from his belt when I nailed him, two in the chest, one in the head. That appeared very pro but I meant to group three in the chest. I only got the headshot because he was falling backward.

A ruckus rose from inside the house: running feet and shouting. No time to run. I wouldn't survive a shootout with a bunch of bad guys at once. I'd been impatient, like always.

I dropped to my knees to cradle the corpse with three new holes in it. Double-plus-dead and laid out flat on the gravel, the tall one was now the long one. I didn't know his name so I decided his post-mortem monicker should be Longfellow.

Three guys rushed out of the front door, guns drawn and eager to kill somebody. They were impatient people, too. Our business was full of them. If we weren't this way, we'd have 401Ks, drive the speed limit and maybe work at a bank.

"They went that way!" I gestured dramatically and begin to cry. "Toward the front gate!" The trick to selling a good cry is to add a wet snort. They'd never think anyone would do that on purpose.

"Who did? Who went where?" the third man bringing up the rear asked in a Cockney accent.

"The killers! Two of them! Guys in black t-shirts and jeans! They're headed for the gate! Quick! They'll get away!"

The dumbest of the trio sprinted in the direction I had pointed. The one that was a little less dumb ran to the Land Rover parked in front of the garage. Gravel flew as his tires spun and he took off in hot pursuit.

Wild goose chase: Engaged. They were gone without giving me another thought.

Bad Guy #3 stopped and stared at me. It dawned on him that he'd never seen me in his life. He was the smartest of the three stooges. I guessed that made him the stooge with the bowl cut. *Moe.* The smartest stooge was named Moe. My dad used to laugh at that silly shit. I didn't get it.

"Where'd you come from?" Moe was armed, but his pistol hung in his hand at his thigh.

Smarter but not smart enough.

My hand was slick with blood when I pulled my pistol out from under the corpse. I pointed it at Moe's head. "*Sh.*"

Moe dropped his weapon in the gravel and backed up. I scooped up the handgun. It was a CZ 75 that fit in my hand nicely. My dad always bought American and disliked guns from the Czech Republic. However, Moe's choice of weapon held sixteen rounds. I didn't know if I would need all that ammo before I was done but the weapon's sleek lethality was a comfort.

I waved Moe toward the front door. He interlaced his fingers behind his head without me having to ask. He didn't say a word and nodded when I told him what to do.

Him, I liked.

I remembered the man I was looking for. I'd met him many times in New York when he was just another thug in the Machine's crew. "Take me to Lonnie."

"Lonnie's not here," Moe said.

"That's a shame. I'm going to have to splatter your brains and slip out the back."

"I could be wrong," he replied. "In fact, I think you'll find him in the panic room."

"Any cameras in there?"

"Um...."

"Answer quick. A man who answers too slow is lying."

"There's a camera outside the panic room, yeah."

"But none out in the yard or in the house?"

"No."

Idiots. Good.

I imagined Lonnie cowering in his panic room. Any minute, he'd call to find out what all the shots were about. As if on cue, Moe's phone rang. He handed it over with no bullshit.

Good boy!

"Lonnie?"

"Who's this?" The guy on the other end of the line was breathing heavily. He sounded big and sweaty.

"Cherry. I've brought the long paper Big Denny De Molina is looking for."

"What's with the gunfire?"

"I had a misunderstanding with your boys. There wasn't a man among them."

"Where's Church? Gimme Church!"

I looked at my captive. "Your name Church?"

He nodded miserably.

"He's right here, Lonnie. Can't come to the phone right now. He's been kneecapped."

"What? How?"

"I showed up with the cash and your guys wanted to take it. That wouldn't be good for me. Big Denny wouldn't like it. Wouldn't be much good for you, either. You should hire a better class of assistants next time."

I gave Lonnie time to get all that nasty cursing out of his system. It took a while. The fact that he was upset only proved me right. His crew was low grade. He wouldn't have believed me so easily otherwise.

Denny sent Lonnie to get his money back but this guy was no boss. He was just another also-ran from New York. Without inspiring respect, any boss could lose control of his crew. Lonnie expected less from his men. Real leaders didn't do that. They expected more. If Big Denny really wanted his money back, he shouldn't have sent the B-team.

"We need a face-to-face," I told Lonnie. "You'll want to get hold of Denny and tell him he's got a lot of his money back, not all of it, but a lot. I'll need you to count out my finder's fee — "

"How do I know you haven't taken out your finder's fee already?"

"Because nobody crosses Big Denny and lives. He's the boss of the Machine and he's much more savage than Vincent Lima ever was. It's been, what? Two years? Still, Denny sent me after that girl. If you owe Denny, he'll find you. It's worse if you make him chase you. Earth's not big enough to play hide-and-seek with Big Denny. He's the elephant who doesn't forget. You should have seen what I did to that bitch. Denny said send a message. There's blood on the floor and hair on the walls."

Lonnie was more scared of Denny than he was of me so he didn't waste time thinking. "C'mon up to the second-floor office, Cherry."

A minute later, I stood upstairs in an office with a desk and a poker table. From the look of things, I'd interrupted a card game. I kept my captive ahead of me as a human shield.

The panic room door opened. Before he emerged, Lonnie called out, "Did you skin that thieving bitch with a carrot peeler like I told you?" He came to a stop when he saw my hostage. The rusty gears in Lonnie's brain began to crank again. "Church? I thought you got kneecapped. What — "

"Oh, right." I shot Church in the right knee. He went down screaming. I pointed the CZ 75 at Lonnie's crotch. "Sorry. That was on my to-do list."

Lonnie stared and his mouth hung open. His mind's gears started to turn faster but they were still pretty creaky. I gave him a minute to catch up. Finally, he said, "You ain't Cherry."

"Good guess. Do you remember me, Lonnie?"

"Lily. I remember. Everybody who's left in the Machine remembers you."

"Good for you," I said. "For a minute there, I thought I was going to have to draw diagrams and explain it with puppets."

"Where's Cherry?"

"Well, I didn't skin her alive with a carrot peeler like she was going to do to me."

"Shit."

"Don't feel too bad for her. She gave you up quick and told me how to find you. She also blabbed that you had only spoken with her on the phone."

"Aw, shit."

"And now here I am, talking to the man who sent that crazy bitch to torture and kill me."

"Aw, shit."

"You're an eloquent guy, Lonnie."

Dad was wrong about always buying American. I loved the feel of the Czech pistol in my hand. Not too much kick in the recoil, either.

4

F orearm skin does not peel the same way a carrot does. Cherry the Ginger Assassin had managed to take some skin off my forearm before I got back in control of the situation. The key to taking down any enemy was to find their weakness.

We all have a fatal flaw. For instance, when I was eight, a girl named Mandy beat me up after school. I don't think it was personal. She was a big girl and had a rep around the school for beating up a lot of kids.

When I came home with a black eye, I complained to my mother. She handed me a bag of ice and told me to learn from the experience.

Outraged at her hands-off parenting style, I demanded, "Learn what?"

"Learn how not to have the experience again."

"How?"

"Find her weakness."

"I was hoping her weakness would be for you to tell her mom and her mom would beat her up."

"If it has to come to that, I'll have to go over to her house and beat her ass and her mother's ass."

"Good."

"No, Lily. No good. You got a problem to solve. How are you going to handle it?"

"Bring a gun to school?"

"That is not a proportionate response. That's a weak-ass way to go. You can do better."

"A stick? A brick?"

"Better than that."

"I don't know, Mom — "

"You're a Vasquez. Do we run from our problems?"

"No."

"What do we do?"

"We run *at* them. But what can I do? She's bigger than me."

"But is she more savage?"

When I didn't answer, Mom told me, "She better not be more savage than you. It's a bad world. If you can't handle a schoolgirl, how are you gonna deal with a real life problem? The world is all business and self-preservation. How you gonna deal with it? You gonna let somebody take your life and your dignity? Life's too important and precious to live like that, baby girl."

I took roundabout ways to get home. My elaborate detours saved me a beating for three days. On the fourth day, my bully caught me again. She threw me to the ground and sat on my head, laughing and demanding money. I discovered, quite by accident, that the insides of the bully's thighs were ticklish. That's how I got out from under my tormentor. Mandy was still on her knees and giggling when I got to my feet. Then I started punching. I had my opening. Between punches, I started screaming, "You think you're bad? You got no idea!"

Some boys from the neighborhood formed a circle around us and laughed as I stopped that girl cold. I kept screaming. My punches were wild and out of control but I kept going, sure that if I let her get to her feet, she'd kill me.

"You're never going to bother me again! Don't even look me in the eyes! Never look me in the eyes! Never!"

Before long, the boys stopped laughing and their concern turned to fear. Some pulled me off her and tried to calm me down. Others ran away and didn't look back.

Mandy lived but she came to school the next day with two black eyes, a swollen purple jaw and a chipped front tooth. She did not look my way. She didn't pick on anybody else, either.

When I came home with bloody knuckles, Mom had the ice pack ready again. She didn't ask what happened to the bully. All she said was, "Next time you punch somebody, put a roll of quarters in your fist."

The Ginger Assassin's fatal flaw was that she enjoyed her job too much. Sadists are careless. They lose sight of the mission with their gory distractions. As she attempted to peel my forearm with a rusty carrot peeler, she stared too long at my blood. It was as if she was thirsty. I guess *bloodthirsty* is a real thing.

When Cherry caught me, I asked myself what Jesus would do. The answer: I begged for my life but I spoke softly, just a whisper. I told her that if she let me go, I'd tell her where all of Big Denny's money was hidden. The window of opportunity was small and I only had one chance. As my captor bent closer, I headbutted the brains out of that psycho bitch.

Cherry held on to the carrot peeler but dropped her gun into my lap. After that, I was the one asking the questions. Never bring a carrot peeler to a gunfight.

Lonnie had his own exploitable flaws. Aside from being a weak leader, he was easily distracted watching Church roll around on the floor.

"Goodnight, Moe." I shot the henchman a couple of times in the chest and he stopped his annoying moaning.

Lonnie paled as he stared at the face of his dying man. I snugged the muzzle of the Czech pistol into Lonnie's crotch. That seemed to cure his ADHD.

I had questions. I got answers. Then I spent more bullets.

Lonnie's burner phone had Big Denny's number on it. Men tasked with killing me and retrieving the skim were dead. Big Denny had waited years to get this close. He was going to be so pissed that he missed this chance.

But trouble doesn't stop coming. The wild goose chasers returned. I heard the Land Rover skid to a stop out front and in a moment both of them pounded around downstairs shouting Lonnie's name and cursing. They checked the house as if they were cops, shouting, "Clear!" for each room they searched. These goons were not smart ninjas.

I tiptoed into a bedroom and took off my shoes. The pair I decided to call Larry and Curly ran upstairs, a couple of freaked-out amateurs. I guess their mothers never taught them how to take care of themselves.

They found the man I'd dubbed Moe and they shouted at each other even more. Then they spotted Lonnie. As blood spread across their boss' crotch and wet brains slid down the wall behind his desk, Larry and Curly's shouts went up an octave. There's something about seeing a man shot in the crotch that bothers men much more than seeing splattered brains. I guess they don't value things they don't use.

Transfixed, the bad guys stood with their backs to me gibbering with adrenalin, not a single cogent thought in their heads. These poor morons were local recruits, definitely new to this sort of thing. I have seen it all before so, soundless in bare feet, I stepped out of the bedroom. They might have been chattering about the price of parrots if Godzilla destroys Tokyo again. Cockney really is impenetrable to me when it's cranking out of an idiot's mouth at full tilt. Creeping closer, I got the gist: Larry and Curly were arguing about who was more to blame for failing to guard Lonnie.

I gripped Lonnie's heavy .38 in my left hand and the CZ 75 in my right. I decided I could solve their argument for them. Both thugs stopped talking when they felt the muzzles on their necks. The CZ 75 pistol was warm. Lonnie's weapon was cold. Both of them went stiff.

"Don't blame yourselves, boys," I said, flat and calm. "You think you're bad? You got no idea."

I dropped them both. Lonnie's gun was too loud in the small space and my ears rang.

5

I was prepared to deal with the aftermath. I really was a Girl Scout, briefly. I liked the little sash but otherwise, the organization's fashion sense did not appeal to me. I stayed with the Scouts long enough to learn to be prepared. I took the weapons and every cell phone.

Mom taught me the utility of savagery.. From Jesus, I learned to improvise on the fly. I found a big gas can in the Land Rover. The corpses in the front yard were too heavy to pull up the stairs so I poured gasoline on Short Round and Longfellow where they fell. Pardon me, I should have said *petrol*.

Ever wondered what it sounds like to torch a mansion? As soon as I dropped the match, the flame was like a rushing wind. The trail of liquid fire raced up the stairs. The fire looked eager. When the flame reached the gas can I had propped on Lonnie's chest, I heard a tinny bang, the shattering of glass and another whoosh as flames burst from the windows.

As the fire spread, the mansion's empty windows glowed like angry orange eyes. It happened faster than I expected. I didn't stay to watch. I did what Jesus would do. I left ashes for the cops to investigate and took off in the Land Rover.

I had to transfer Lonnie's data to my cell and dump the rest of the phones. I couldn't keep the getaway vehicle for long but I put some distance between me and the mansion. Surely someone would soon notice a funeral pyre the size of a huge house. As I pulled onto the street, I counted the cost: Longfellow, Short Round, Church AKA Moe, Larry, Curly and Lonnie.

I'd become the assassin who'd tried to torture and murder me for one night. Only when I was safely on the road and away did my hands begin to shake. I can't say it was all terrible. Playing the Ginger Assassin was empowering. I'm not crazy, though (or at least I'm still sane enough to know I shouldn't feel good about it). My breath came in little gasps.

I'd taken the money to escape New York and make a better life. In the scheme of sins, theft was a smaller sin than murder. You could even call it self-defense and, unless you're Amish or something, pretty much everybody's for self-defense. This was business and self-preservation.

Those were seven killers who would have killed me if I'd given them a chance. I would not weep for them but my hands continued to shake as I drove away from my sins. I yanked the red wig off and swore I'd never be a ginger again.

Many blocks away, I was still thinking about the surprised look on Lonnie's face when I pulled the trigger. As adrenaline burned off, my exhaustion began to set in. I couldn't wait to escape into sleep. I ditched the car and cleaned myself up. I had rags and alcohol in the duffel. Like a good Girl Scout, I came prepared. A long walk and two cabs later, I got back to my flat.

In the dim light coming in from the streetlight, I spotted two things wrong with my small living room. There were two bodies. When I left, there had been only one.

Cherry's corpse lay on the floor. I was more worried about the silhouette of the man slumped in my gaming chair. I pulled out Lonnie's piece and aimed it at him. "Who's been sleeping in my — " I didn't finish my Goldilocks joke.

The man awoke and looked up. The light struck his face as he smiled down the barrel of the .38. It was as if he looked Death in the face every day. His sharp eyes fixed on mine and he smiled wider. "Hi, Lily."

"*Jesus*, Jesus!" The first Jesus was the popular hippie deity. The second Jesus was pronounced, "Hay-soose."

Jesus Diaz rose from the chair. I lowered the weapon. He pulled me into his arms and we stood there a moment. Coming together felt familiar and natural, like the best of the old times. I felt a little safer in his presence. Jesus is the only man I've ever known, besides my father, who was determined not to disappoint me.

Seeing him again, I remembered all the drama in New York too well. There was the car explosion that still haunted my dreams, for instance. To come this far, I had to shoot a Romanian gangster in the head. My life had become cleansed of all that. Playing video games, admiring architecture and painting like Salvador Dali was all I wanted to do. I didn't want the old times back but I had missed Jesus Diaz.

He pointed to Cherry's corpse. "You going to introduce me to your friend? I've been sitting here a while. She's a lousy conversationalist. All I know is that Denny sent her."

"Nah. She was taking a census. I hate when strangers come door to door."

He allowed a tight smile. "Are you done?"

"Jesus Diaz, meet Cherry something AKA the Ginger Assassin."

"Ha-ha."

"No, really, that's what she called herself."

"Hard to imagine she thought that was cool."

"Maybe she called herself that ironically."

"Like some kind of hipster assassin?"

"Don't judge. Most of the guys you came up with took their cues on how to act from *Goodfellas*."

"Still one of the best movies ever."

Same old Jesus. Thank God.

"It's good to see you, Lily. How's that new life working out for you?"

"It was great until very recently."

"What's your plan?"

"To keep my new life. Normal is nice. We used to make fun of nice but nice is very nice. Boring is underrated."

"Oh," he said. "Sorry, Lily, but I seriously doubt that's something you can sustain."

6

"I missed you by two days in Madrid," Jesus said.

I looked him up and down. We used to go to clubs almost every night. He was a great dancer, kind of a pretty boy then. Jesus looked tougher around the edges than the last time I saw him, as if he'd been in a few more fights that didn't go well. Rugged suited him. "How long have you been looking for me?"

"Not long. I got shot."

"Where?"

"In Hollywood."

"No, I mean where?" I gestured at his the length of his body.

"They missed my dick and brain so I'm okay. I took it in the side. I've been out of circulation for a while. Had to recover."

"My god! Are you okay?"

"I am now."

I hugged him and we were quiet for a moment. I wasn't sure how much more I should ask.

"It wasn't like the movies," he added. "It hurt more than I thought it would and it took longer to get over it than I expected."

"Who did it?"

"Doesn't matter. They're on another celestial plane now. Hey, you know the man from Miami I always wanted to find?"

I almost laughed. The man from Miami killed Jesus' mother and brother. Nobody forgets a story like that. "You found him?"

"He found me. Long story short, that story's over. I'm moving on after I tie up a few loose ends. That's how I ended up looking for you, actually."

"You said you tried to catch me in Madrid. Is that what I am now? A loose end?"

"No, I tried to catch *up* to you in Madrid. Big difference."

"Do you need money? I could help — "

"The money is the problem, not the solution. Denny wants whatever is left of the skim."

"He sent you after me, too?"

"His people patched me up in Mexico. You're my first job. I owe him so — "

"So you and Denny are tight again? After he tried to have you killed?"

"We nearly killed each other. I haven't forgotten. I agreed to a truce that serves our mutual interests. I talked my way out, played on his nostalgia for the bad old days when we lived on the street. I was hoping to buy you time." He glanced toward the corpse of my would-be assassin. "Somebody got impatient."

"Denny's not about friendship. He's all about the money."

Jesus shrugged. "And we're not? I chased Panama Bob out on a high ledge to get the skim."

I sighed. Jesus owed Denny. I owed Jesus. "If you want the money, I'll give it to you."

He shook his head. "I'd take that deal if I thought that could end the chase but we stole from the Machine, Lily. In the end, Denny will kill us whether we give the money back or not. You might as well keep it."

My gaze strayed back to the dead woman. "The money has kept me alive. If Cherry didn't have questions about where it was, she could have just shot me and that would be it. Denny is so fulla shit.

He'll send somebody else. This will never end until I'm dead. It's been years since I left New York. Why all this now?"

Jesus shrugged. "Denny seems to be doing alright but looks can be deceiving. Maybe he needs the money for something special. He could be cashing in his chips for a big move on someone else's territory."

"Or it's just about pride," I said. "There was always somebody looking to climb the Machine's ladder."

"Letting you gallivant across the world on the mob's dime is seen as weakness, not mercy. He can't forget you."

"I am unforgettable."

In a beat of silence, he appraised me. "You are memorable, that's true. You look great, Lily. Despite the circumstances, it is good to see you. I never thought I'd see you again."

It was sweet of him to say. However, a dead woman was in my living room and I'd just committed mass murder, arson and car theft. I might have missed a stop sign back in August, too. I was not in the mood for compliments.

Jesus could read my moods like no other so he got back to business. "What were you going to do with the body?"

"Not sure. She'd make a nice lamp. Maybe a planter?"

"Lily."

"She didn't just try to kill me, Jesus. She tortured me." I pulled my sleeve back and showed him the bandage on my forearm.

He frowned. "First priority, let's change that dressing."

"And then?"

"We've got to get rid of that." He pointed to Cherry. "Rigor mortis has set in. We have to wait until that's over before we can move her. We have to get out of here, too."

"I like this flat. The water in the shower is always too cold, but — "

"Denny knows where you are. We have to erase your trail. I would have you packed and gone already if not for the Ginger Assassin."

"How did you know I'd come back?"

"Your clothes were all here and there's that suitcase full of money in the crawlspace."

"You've been busy."

"Time invested in reconnaissance is seldom wasted."

"I hope you didn't bother my downstairs neighbor."

"I checked. She was out. By the pictures on the walls, she's a nice old-fashioned girl. She dusts. I don't know anybody our age or younger who dusts, do you? I don't even have a regular job but I don't dust. Who has that kind of time?"

"My neighbor *is* nice. Her name's Denise. She's got a job she seems to like. The day I moved in, she invited me for tea. She's a bookkeeper now but she is studying to become an accountant. She's on the hunt for a nice girl to settle down with. She had her heart set on me for a while but I had to turn her down. Denise hasn't invited me back for more tea since the day I turned her down. That's kind of irritating."

Jesus smiled. "You're not a nice girl?"

"Denise is a girl who doesn't know how the real world works. I keep my distance from the Normies. If somebody like Cherry came along and thought I had a friend, she might try to use a friend against me. I don't know Denise well but I admire the life she's making for herself. Her existence seems boring but boring is peaceful, right?"

"You sound like you might envy her a little."

"I do, a little, but people like us can't fit into the Normie life."

"Peaceful does sound nice," Jesus agreed.

"It's unreachable. For people like us, their lives are entirely theoretical. Trouble always finds us."

Jesus looked away for the first time. "We do have a knack, don't we? Might be our fault, huh?"

"Might be."

7

"Why did you feel it was necessary to break into Denise's apartment, too?"

"Break is a bit strong. Your downstairs neighbor keeps a key under the flower pot. I wanted to make sure none of the blood under that stiff seeped through your floor to her ceiling. You should be more careful."

I quirked an eyebrow at him. "Oh, look, Practical Jesus is here."

"I'm not scolding, I'm sharing. Next time put down some plastic."

"I didn't know trouble was coming until I woke up in bed with that bitch sitting on top of me. At first, I thought it was Denise from downstairs getting all handsy and proactive."

"But you figured out it wasn't Denise before you killed her, right?"

"Obviously. I'm not a monster. I only do monstrous things when necessary."

"Okay, then." I wasn't sure he believed me but, given his history, he was in no position to throw stones at my glass house.

"How long you been here?" I ask.

"Not long. I think I slept for a while before you showed up."

"Did you go through everything I own?"

"I couldn't guess the password on the computer, but yeah, pretty much. Love the underwear. I didn't know Frederick's of Hollywood was still a thing but — "

I slapped him hard. A bitch slap is mostly the fingers. I got my palm into it so he rocked back on his heels a little.

It had to sting but Jesus made a show of being unperturbed. "If the Ginger Assassin had been smarter, she'd have found your stash while you were out. She could have waited behind your bedroom closet door to kill you, no fuss, plenty of muss."

"Is that what you would have done?"

"If I was doing what Denny asked, I would have been waiting in the closet, yeah. I'm on your side. Always. You know that, right?"

I knew. I was so sure I didn't even have to answer. Jesus always understood me.

"I don't want to be in the killing business anymore, Lily."

"Oh? How did that happen?"

"I worked security for a while. Protecting people was pretty good while it lasted. I'd like to do that again, if you'll let me. I liked being a bodyguard before it turned to shit."

"Sounds like you failed as a bodyguard."

"I lost a friend. The past caught up with me the same way it's catching up with you. Tell me the truth: Is the money in the suitcase all that's left of the Machine's money?"

"No. That's just cash on hand."

Even in the dim light, I could read him well, too. He looked relieved.

"Surprised? I'm more thrifty than you think," I said. "I don't buy much and when I do, I'm the queen of the thrift shop treasure hunt." I gestured at the nearly bare apartment and Jesus gave me a little nod, conceding the point.

I added, "I was always thriftier than you, Mr. Armani-or-Nothing."

Jesus still wore a sharp suit and those ridiculously expensive shoes. He shrugged and nodded again and I suddenly realized I was acting like a bitch. I would never have escaped New York alive with the skim if it weren't for all that Jesus did for me. He almost died for my sins. "Sorry about the slap."

"Wh-what? Was that an apology? That might be unprece-dented. Is there a pod in the backyard?"

I gave him a grim smile. "Yes, that was an apology. And I don't get that reference. I presume it's a movie." Jesus was always obsessed with movies.

"*Invasion of the Body* — you know what? Never mind. It was a stupid joke. Apology accepted. Sorry I went through your stuff."

"I understand. You were trying to figure out what was going on with me."

"That and I did want to see your underwear drawer."

"The back of my hand is getting itchy, Jesus. You want another slap? I'll put some knuckles in it — "

Jesus held up both hands, showing me his empty palms. "Take it easy. When I picked your lock and found a dead woman in the dark, at first I thought it was you. I went a little crazy until I turned the lights on."

"I'm the same, but calmer ... or at least I was until I had to take a trip to Camberley."

Jesus nodded toward my easel in the corner of the room. "Nice painting, by the way."

My attempt to emulate Dali's style in *The Temptation of St. Anthony* was only a quarter of the way done and now I had to bug out. I couldn't take my painting or my gaming computer with me. Jesus was right, I had been too careless. "What would you have done if it was me dead?"

"Gone all *Kill Bill* and slaughtered everyone with a samurai sword."

"Didn't see that one, either."

"Lily! It's *Tarantino!* You saw Uma Thurman be badass with me. Remember? You wanted her yellow Bruce Lee tracksuit." Jesus Christ has his religion. Jesus Diaz worships movies.

"Kidding," I said. "We went to see the *Kill Bill* marathon at the Film Forum on Houston. Before the show, you and Denny dragged me into that antique place down the street filled with guns and swords."

"Back when Denny was your friend," he said.

"And he was like a brother to you."

"He was, but what's over is over. He won't stop coming after us," Jesus said. "So you better bring me up to speed on everything."

We stared at each other a moment. We were magnets, pulled together by the force of attraction. I began to tell him a little of what happened in Camberley. Then the floodgates opened and I spilled everything, blow by blow, death by death. My voice trembled and tremors jangled through my body. My adrenaline dump was over and I was relatively safe. That was my body's cue to finally go into shock.

Jesus called the response "after action." He held me tighter and rubbed my back hard. I couldn't get warm but I kept speaking, confessing everything. When I finished, he said nothing. He just held me.

Nothing was exactly the right thing to say. Holding me was the right thing to do. We'd been apart for a long time but standing together beside a corpse, it felt like a new beginning, but not necessarily the beginning of anything good.

8

M y mother once told me a story about moving a body. "Your father had to break the arms and legs with a hammer to get that tub of lard into a freezer."

Mom always had the best stories but I couldn't share them with anyone. I didn't imagine any of my mother's best stories would be received well over coffee after yoga class or at a book club. Her tales often ended with, "And we didn't have to deal with that deserving fool again."

My mother seemed to have spent her life preparing me for mine. Most of the other children of gangsters were encouraged to go to university. Dad wanted to keep me out of the underground economy. Mom always figured I was bound for the family business. (We kept that a secret from him, too.)

If this were America, we could have stashed the Ginger Assassin's body in a big freezer. I didn't have one and besides, almost everything, including the household appliances, is smaller in Europe. We rolled the body in a sheet of plastic Jesus picked up from a nearby construction site.

"In the future, try not to kill anyone at home," Jesus advised as he cleaned up blood with a sponge. While I showered, he had popped out to get cleaning supplies. "One or two more bodies and you'll have to admit it's a habit."

I was annoyed but, to be fair, I had killed someone in my apartment before. That was my first murder back in my New York life. I crushed that deserving fool's skull with a cast-iron skillet. We never heard from him again, either.

"My atrocities have roared back and chased me across the ocean," I told Jesus. "I should have flown to Fiji. Now look at me, working a mop."

Safe within the Machine, my family used to have minions to dispose of bodies. Someone else took care of getting rid of my deserving fool. I did miss that about New York. That and the pizza.

Jesus pointed with his chin at the bucket of bloody water. "A broom and a dustpan won't do the job. The good news is the floor is hardwood. Rugs are hell to clean. If you get blood in a rug, it's always in the fibers. You have to rip it up."

"Noted for future reference."

"You want to start on that blood spatter on the wall?"

"Not desperately, but I will."

"Don't forget the ceiling, either."

Curious to see if I'd made national news yet, I reached for the remote. Jesus lunged to snatch it away. "Don't watch TV, Lily."

"Why not?"

"Trust me. I've been down this road. After something big goes down, never watch the news. It gets into your head if you see cops crawling all over a crime scene. You got away. They have no solid leads. Don't make it more complicated. The news will only be guesswork and misinformation, anyway."

"I had an idea in the shower," I said. "What if we pin the whole mess on Cherry? Suppose this corpse turned up. Wouldn't the cops be quick to put what happened in Camberley on gangland escapades? Case solved and they're done and happy, right?"

He looked skeptical. "This isn't home, Lily. When a bunch of people die here, it's really big."

"Can't you see the headline? Ginger Assassin, the crazed killer who went nuts in Camberley — "

Jesus shook his head.

"Why not? I was impersonating her, red wig and all — "

"The forensics won't work. Between gunpowder residue, body decomposition, no smell of gas on her — "

I let out a long sigh. Jesus used to be a cop in the military. He didn't think cops are as stupid as I hoped they were.

"Okay, How about this?" I asked. "I could do the rogue assassin gets greedy thing. I've got Denny's number. I could impersonate Cherry on the phone. Suppose I tell Denny that Lily Vasquez is dead and he can stop looking. Then I disappear so Cherry disappears, her to hell and me to Fiji."

"If we could make the body disappear permanently, maybe that could work."

"Sure, it would. Makes sense. Cherry disappears with Denny's money. Problem solved. When he comes looking, he's chasing a ghost."

I let Jesus think about it as I poured a pail of bloody water down the sink in the kitchen. I replaced it with clean water as he pondered the idea.

When I looked up from scrubbing the wall, Jesus was leaning against the door frame and nodding. "The only way Denny stops looking for you is if you're dead. He'll call to tell me my girlfriend is dead —"

"Ex-girlfriend."

"Then he'll tell me to chase down Cherry. We could run up my expense account in Paris or Turkey or Japan for a while before I give up. Sounds fun, right?"

"Did you hear what I said? *Ex*-girlfriend."

"We're different people now, aren't we? Time's passed. Before you write us off, we should see if we click. We clicked before — "

"You remember what Big Denny called you?"

"He called me lots of things. Not much that I could repeat in front of anybody's mom if their mom goes to church."

"Silver-tongued devil. I haven't forgotten. I appreciate your help, Jesus, but you're not talking me into your dreams of white picket fences and babies."

"Nah, I'm Captain Logical now. You know what I've done and I know what you've done. We're both still here instead of running away screaming. We're not normal, Lily. We've seen too much for that. Neither of us is going to wind up as a bookkeeper whose only adventure is hitting on the hot Latina in the upstairs flat over tea and a scone."

"Sadly, Denise had no scones. Too bad. That might have closed the deal. I might have reconsidered, at least. I'm flexible."

9

Miami and circumstance made Jesus Diaz the way he was. New York and family made me what I am. We recognized the broken parts of ourselves in each other. Basking in the warm glow of the Non-Normal Club, we'd become friends and lovers.

I'd just confessed to killing a bunch of people. Jesus hadn't blinked. He understood why I did what I did. He accepted that my reasons were sound. He didn't pepper me with a thousand questions and judgments. I could burn through all of Christian Mingle, JDate and Tinder and not find that level of understanding. Some psychos on Craigslist might get a freak like me but kindred spirits are rare.

As if he read my mind, Jesus added, "We know the game."

As I scrubbed up blood and wrung the sponge into a bucket again, I wished I were more like Denise. Call it a moment of weakness. "Is there something extra wrong with us, do you think? Could we be normal, if we pretended?"

"Like method acting, you mean? I don't know if that would stick."

I must have looked crestfallen. His grim face softened. "We're on the side of the angels, Lily. The law would never catch Denny's guys and people like us can't call a cop to solve our problems. Cops are for after the damage is done. When I was in the military police, I can't think of many examples of preventing a crime. Pulling over drunk drivers on base before they wiped out a family was pretty solid, I guess. That's about it."

"So it's decided," I said. "I'll call Denny, tell him I'm dead and set him on the crazy bitch's trail. After we find a way to get rid of her."

"So she'll never be found, yeah."

"Or at least until Denny's dead."

Jesus shifted back and forth uncomfortably. He got what I was hinting at.

"Death wipes out debt, Jesus. Mom used to say that's the one thing that's civil about the mob. When civilians die they still have to worry about taxes and lawyers. The government doesn't give up on trying to get paid after you're dead and cold. With the Machine, you die, you don't owe and you are not owed. If I take Denny out and he's not the one slinging orders anymore — "

"Lily, if you want to be closer to normal, don't turn into Denny De Molina. You don't want that."

"Don't I?"

"I hope you don't. Besides, whoever replaced him would want the skim, too. And you dead."

I said nothing and looked around the flat. I'd miss this place. My gaze fell on my computer. It was the gaming rig I'd built by myself. I had been very budget conscious for a long time before I decided to splurge $2,500 on the graphics card. I worried I'd have to leave my system behind, but maybe I could put the computer in storage until I took Big Denny out of the game. For Jesus, taking on Denny was Plan Z. To me, murdering the Machine's boss sounded like a decent Plan A. Jesus was a nostalgic kind of guy. I decided not to tell him.

"We should come up with a script for when you impersonate Cherry," Jesus suggested. "After he sends me on the hunt, I'll tell him I found your body. I'll cry a lot, on cue. Then I'll swear vengeance on the elusive Ginger Assassin. When the heat dies down, how about I meet you somewhere?"

"Seriously? That doesn't sound safe."

"We'll get to know each other all over again and start fresh."

"Like normal people?"

"Like you said, maybe if we pretend it will take — "

"I want to go back to Madrid."

"*Mm* ... too soon. Go someplace no one would expect. Go to Finland."

"How expensive is bandwidth there? And wait, why Finland? Sounds cold and fish-oriented. I want a place that sounds less wintery and more fun. How about a fun land instead of Finland? Like uh...the Dominican Republic? Or Costa Rica? *Then* Fiji."

"Too small. Do Finland. I read somewhere it's the happiest place on Earth ... or the one with the most alcoholism and suicides, I forget which."

"Finland?" I couldn't believe what I was hearing.

"Call it penance for your sins," he said. "Finland is the perfect hiding place. When I suggested it, you made that face you make, like when you tried sauerkraut for the first time. I guarantee, no one will look for you there."

I considered whipping my wet bloody sponge at him.

Jesus checked the view from the window. When he turned back, he looked concerned. "There's a car parked across the street. The guy's just sitting there. He's been there a while, like since I came back with the cleaning stuff."

"Meaning?"

"It means he's indiscreet. Plan A is out the window. The Ginger Assassin came here without ID or keys. My first guess is that's her ride."

"What's Plan B?"

"I have no idea yet."

I had a bad feeling, no, a certainty. I definitely would not be able to take my gaming tower with me. However, I determined one thing: Big Denny De Molina would not make me run and hide in fucking Finland. Denny and Jesus had called a truce but to me, the new capo of the Machine was just another deserving fool.

10

I had a backpack stuffed with clothes and money — mostly money. I could always buy more clothes.

We slipped out into the garden. That's something I like about England. People call their backyards "gardens." I wondered if British jails are more genteel than the Supermax prisons in the States. Would there be tea and scones at four beside tennis courts made of grass? Probably not.

Nobody was waiting to arrest or murder us. I told Jesus we had to run, but he had more proactive ideas. He took my hand as if it was old times when we were a couple of kids in love. I haven't felt young since I was a little kid who didn't know what her dad did for a living.

We walked around a long block until we circled behind the car Jesus had spotted.

"What if he's a cop?"

"If he was a cop, he wouldn't be alone. They'd have the place surrounded and the block locked down."

"I have a feeling we should be running for our lives."

"Right now we're just walking fast for our lives," he said.

"You think it's one of Denny's guys — "

"I'm supposed to be Denny's guy. We can use that."

Jesus pulled me into a doorway as if we were making out. As we embraced, I scanned the street. All quiet. No other players seemed to be in this game.

Jesus suddenly looked grimmer. "What if *I* was followed?"

"You know how to spot a tail and lose one."

"I might be out of practice."

"Maybe he's waiting for someone else. Maybe he's hoping for a hooker to wander by."

"Are there still streetwalkers anymore? Hasn't all sex gone digital? I mean dating apps, not digital like using your finger."

"What are you, twelve?"

"I'm on the dirty side of thirty. Never thought I'd last this long."

He held me tight again, his breath hot in my ear. "I'll check out the car. If this guy is wrong, I'll make him right."

"How?"

"Somehow. This is fucked up. Let's unfuck it."

Jesus headed for the car. When he rapped on the driver's window, the guy startled a little. He'd been half-asleep.

I couldn't allow Jesus to deal with this problem alone. I walked up to the other side of the car and pulled out Lonnie's .38. It was a good thing I did. Just at that moment a guy in the back seat rose up holding a sawed-off shotgun and pointed it at Jesus. I didn't wait and I didn't think. I pulled the trigger. That big roscoe bucked in my fist and splattered brains and bone across the rear windshield with one shot.

Frozen in fear, the driver looked back at me. When he turned back, the muzzle of Jesus' SIG 226 was in his face. Jesus looked over the car's roof at me and shook his head in exasperation. "Too Tarantino, babe. *Way too* Tarantino. That was so *Pulp Fiction*."

"You're welcome."

I looked left and right. No one on the street, but someone could have been dialing 999 as we stood there. If we didn't get out soon it could have turned into a fox hunt.

"Denny send you?" Jesus asked the driver.

"Who?"

"How'd you find me?"

The guy's voice shook. "I go where I'm told, mister. The bloke in the back told me where to go and — "

"You're lying. That's often a smart move in this business but not today and not with me."

"I swear to God, I'm telling the truth! I only wanted to make a few extra quid and that man …" He gulped hard and began to sob.

The driver was covered in gore and, when he tried to wipe his eyes, he realized how much dead guy was plastered all over him. The driver blubbered and muttered unintelligibly and I suddenly felt bad. I came around the car and I clicked my tongue, tapping the windshield with the .38. Under the glass was an Uber sticker. The driver was telling the truth.

Jesus had one Golden Rule: Thou shalt not kill civilians.

11

Jesus bent from the waist so he was eye level with the driver. "Listen."

"I'm sorry, sir. I — "

"I said *listen*. Are you a good listener?"

The driver nodded.

"Has the mess in your back seat got a name?"

"H-he called himself Mr. Black."

"Okay. Where'd you pick him up?"

"The Savoy. He gave me a hundred quid for the night and said I'd get another hundred at the end."

"To follow me."

"Aye."

"Fine." Jesus looked at me. "Cover him a minute."

I stuck the .38 in the driver's face and put a finger to my lips. "*Sh.*"

As I strained to hear the sing-song *la-la, la-la* of sirens, Jesus opened the car's back door and leaned in. I could tell he was trying not to get any blood on him. Good luck with that.

When he straightened, Jesus held the sawed-off shotgun, ammo and a roll of bills wrapped in a rubber band. The bloody back seat and the wad reminded me of *Pulp Fiction*. We watched the movie so many times, Jesus must have worn that DVD out.

He was right. This situation was way too Tarantino. Maybe if I had warned Mr. Black I was behind him, things would have gone down differently. We would never know now. My mother taught me that survival is about making do and dealing with what you've got, not wishing problems away. If she were here, she'd have shot the Uber driver already and we'd have been on our way.

Jesus pushed past me and dug into the driver's jacket. for his wallet. In the cast of the streetlight, he peered at the man's ID. "Okay, Wade Finnegan, I know where you live."

"Oh, sweet *Jaysus!*" the driver said.

Jesus counted out a bunch of bills and handed me roughly half the money. I stuffed it in my bra so I wouldn't have to fumble around with my pistol. Both men give me a long look and I lasered my ex with a hard look so he knew to stay on task. *No boob jokes.*

"You married, Wade?" Jesus asked.

"No."

"Girlfriend?"

"No."

"Dry spell, huh? You live with anyone?"

"No, sir."

Jesus nodded and crouched so he was eye level with the driver again. "Wade. Eyes on me."

I recognized that look. Jesus was doing his Chili Palmer impression. He loved John Travolta in *Get Shorty* even more than he loved the actor in *Pulp Fiction*.

"See this woman? She doesn't care for loose ends. She didn't hesitate to blast Mr. Black, and she wants to kill you, too. I will suggest a solution in which you get to continue to eat, breathe and masturbate to raunchy German porn. What do you say? Sound better than a bullet in the head? Bullets in the head don't always go as well as you think. Sometimes it takes a while to die even with a head wound. I know that sounds weird but it does happen occasionally and — "

"Anything you say, sir!" Finnegan looked at Jesus Diaz like he was the Second Coming.

Jesus glanced over the man's driver's license again. "You're pretty malnourished, aren't you, Wade? What are you? A buck twenty?"

"A what?"

"He's asking how much you weigh," I said.

"Nine stone, about."

Jesus looked to me for help. He was always lousy at math. Whenever we went out, I had to calculate the tip.

I sighed. "He's 126 pounds."

"Okay. That will work. Here's how this is going to play out. See that house across the street? You will park your car in the back alley and leave it there. Take the plates and anything that ties you to these wheels. You got a screwdriver, Wade?"

"In the boot, yeah, a full toolkit."

"Just a screwdriver for the plates, Wade. You'll go up to the second-floor flat in that house across the street. You will have a shower. That place is a crime scene so you will have to be careful. You will leave no trace that you were there. Leave no fingerprints. Wipe down whatever you touch — "

"I have gloves in the boot. I could wear those."

"Excellent, Wade. I like you. You're going to get through this just fine as long as you follow the plan. Be thorough and when you're done, put your clothes in a plastic bag. You'll find garbage bags in the apartment. Change into whatever clothes fit. I'm sure you'll find something passable. T-shirt and jeans will do. Stay out of the lacy underwear drawer."

I was tempted to shoot them both and be done with it. Instead, I tapped my foot and gave Jesus my darkest evil eye.

"You'll dump that bag somewhere far from home where no one will find it," Jesus continues. "Toss the plates. Choose a place that is different from where you ditch the bloody clothes, the Thames maybe. Whatever. You with me so far?"

"I think so."

"You think so or you know so?"

"I know so, sir."

"That's good, Wade, very good. You will then take public transportation to someplace where it's another long walk home. Stay away from people and major streets as much as you can. When you get home, you will change into your own clothes and you're going to take one more walk. Whatever clothes you took from the apartment across the street, you will ditch those, too."

"I understand." The driver nodded vigorously.

"You were never here. No one you know can see you or they're going to be in deep shit, too. By sometime early tomorrow morning, you'll go to bed and be glad you're alive and well. Sleep as long as you like. When you wake up, your car won't be where you thought it was. You'll be shocked. You'll report it stolen. You'll be upset, but deep down, you'll know this nightmare will be over. You never saw us. People forget all sorts of things. Our faces? That's something to forget and never breathe a word. Take this memory to the grave, Wade. You could live a long time or you could be in an unmarked grave before midnight tomorrow. Read me?"

"Yeah. Yes, I do, sir."

"Good man. Now repeat every step back to us or my lovely friend will shoot you in the face."

Wade Finnegan stuttered a lot, but he repeated the play back to us. He added, "What about my wallet and my ID?"

"Good thinking, Wade. You left that in the car. It was in the glove compartment. That's another reason you'll be so upset when you report your vehicle stolen."

Jesus handed him the rest of Mr. Black's money. "Keep this in a safe spot. Don't keep it where you live. Bury it, maybe. Spend none of it for a while. Sound fair?"

A car passed us, sweeping us with its headlights but, lucky for everyone, they moved on.

"Hey, Wade," I said. "Are you picking up what my man is putting down? Are you absolutely sure you smell what he's cooking'?"

Wade nodded, his eyes on the mouth of the .38.

I leaned in, close enough to smell the blood all over him. "If you go wrong on this, I *will* show up behind you someday. You don't doubt that, am I right?"

Wade nodded hard.

I told myself the driver's compliance should make no difference. By the time he had a chance to screw us over, I expected to have escaped to someplace far away. I just hoped that place was not going to be Finland.

12

W e were about to walk away when Jesus paused and turned back to the driver. "Hey, man. Uber is a tough gig. Think about using that money to get yourself out from under, huh? There's got to be easier ways to make money. Find 'em."

"Thank you, sir." The driver sounded as if he meant it.

"You're welcome, Wade. You're handling this right. The worst is already over. Imagine what else you could handle if you put your mind to it." Jesus made the sign of the cross, blessing Wade Finnegan before we walked away.

"What was that, at the end?" I asked. "I got him pissing himself and you talk to him like this is a motivational seminar. Who are you? Tony Robbins?"

"I've never been to a seminar, but I've listened to a bunch of Tony Robbins on audio."

"What?"

"I'm working on myself."

"Working on yourself? That doesn't sound like my Jesus."

He shrugged. "Got shot, remember? Makes a man think about the big picture. I'm still Jesus, but I'm Jesus two-point-oh. I'm setting my mind to new possibilities. Now that I've survived getting shot, I'm wondering if there's more to life than mere survival. Intimidation tactics can only get you so far. You need to hit these sorts of problems from all angles to make sure the play breaks the way you want. A stick is useful, but add a carrot and everybody feels solid about the deal."

"Solid? Solid would have been shooting him in the head and leaving it at that."

"He's a civilian, Lily."

"Mom would have shot him."

"The harder solution was more satisfying, wasn't it?"

"That's a pretty mature stance for a guy who blows up buildings."

Jesus cleared his throat and gave me a meaningful look. "Don't go picking up my bad habits. Oh, right, you already have."

"When I burned down that mansion, I was just trying to survive, same as you."

"Rampages draw too much heat. Better to be subtle when you can."

"You're the wrong person to give that lecture, Jesus. I might have to be a little crazy sometimes, but my crazy saved your life, remember?"

"I remember." He whirled and kissed me. It was soft and slow and when he pulled back he stared in my eyes. "Thanks."

"For saving you?"

"That. And for kissing me back."

"Get over it. We've got business. What's next?"

"We have to hurry to the Savoy."

"For?"

"Don't worry. No time for naked hijinks. Mr. Black is — was — in the same hotel."

"Fine."

"I recognized him."

"What?"

"The guy in the back seat. There was enough of his face left on one side. I remember him from Washington Heights."

"Oh. Who?"

"Luca…something. I forget his last name. Older guy. He ran a numbers game in the old days."

"I don't remember a Luca Something."

"He was part of the Machine, but low-level."

"You wasted all the high-level guys. I guess Denny moved him up."

"Guess so. You okay?"

"Yeah, why?"

"You're trembling."

"I just killed a guy, but only because I had to."

"You're handling it pretty well."

"But?"

"But now you've killed a man with a name. It's harder when they aren't some anonymous goon."

"No, I'm fine."

"You sure? It should be hard — "

I rolled my eyes. "The more I know about these guys, the easier it is to pull the trigger. Isn't that the way it is for you?"

He shook his head. "I wasn't talking about me."

"You never do. So? Does it make a difference to you, knowing their names?"

He paused for so long I didn't think he was going to open up. Then he said, "In hockey fights, they got a rule."

"Not a hockey fan."

"Me neither. The rule is, the ref will let you fight, but if you're gonna throw bones, you gotta drop the gloves. That never made sense to me. I mean, yeah, with those big gloves they could kill each other…but if I'm mad enough to fight, I'm not pulling off the gloves or holding back. If it comes to a fight, I will kill the other guy before he kills me. When I do that without getting killed, I usually feel good. For me, I want to know who I killed and I want him to be everything that's wrong with the world. That way, when I turn out his lights, I'm making the world a better place."

"I get what you're saying but he's just as dead either way."

Jesus nodded. "Thanks for taking out the guy in the back seat. Mr. Black almost got me. You did the right thing by not hesitating."

"I know."

He smiled and put an arm around me. "You learned that from me."

I shrugged him off. "I learned that from my mother."

"Oh. Heh. How is the Momster?"

"Fine, last I heard. I haven't heard for a while. I'd forgotten you called her Momster."

"She thought that was cute. Didn't catch on that I meant 'monster.'"

"Oh, she knew but she thought it was funny."

"*Hmph.* And you? Are you turning into a monster, Lily?"

"Things were peaceful for a long while but this isn't my first day in the slaughterhouse," I said. "I'm used to the blood. You think there's a difference between us and monsters?"

"Monsters enjoy the slaughter," Jesus said.

"And we're just trying to see tomorrow."

He was quiet for a time. By the time I thought the conversation was over, he said, "I like that answer."

"We never talked about this stuff when we were together," I said.

"We should have. I didn't think of you as a killer then, though."

"You were too much in your head. You never let me in. You treated me like a princess."

"You are a princess."

"I'm a warrior princess. You should have let me in, talked about the job ... and about what happened in Miami."

"I didn't know any other girls who could handle all that." He pointed at his head. "It's dark in there."

"I could have handled it, sure. You never gave me the chance."

Jesus shut up. I liked him more for not arguing. We walked for a long time. At first, we were getting away from the crime scene. When we turned a corner to a busy street, we blended in. Then we were just us.

When I took his hand, we looked like any other couple on the street in London in autumn. I could almost forget who I was. It was a shame I'd have to run away and never come back.

For a few glorious minutes I was not Lily Vasquez, daughter of a mobbed-up guy in the Machine. I let go of all the blood and grudges. I remembered what good felt like.

Mom always said good doesn't last so I grab it while I can. Civilians would expect me to get all teary about the carnage but my mother taught me something else: If my enemies were horizontal and I was vertical, that didn't make me a bad person.

It made me the winner, Momster approved.

13

A t The Savoy, Jesus flashed his key and smiled at the clerk at the front desk. He still had blood on his pants so I stood in front of him.

The clerk wore a name tag that told us his name was Stanley. The lenses of his glasses were so thick, his eyes appeared as huge as a cartoon frog. Stanley tried to be discreet but stole glances my way every few seconds. I subtly undid another button on my blouse and moved closer to lean on the front counter. I leaned just so and the countertop pushed the girls together better than a push-up bra, like an offering. We didn't have to worry about the clerk spotting the blood on my ex's pants. Jesus could have been on fire and Stanley would have still been peering down my blouse.

"Could you help us out, Stanley?" Jesus asked. "A friend of mine should be booked in by now. We're supposed to meet for dinner this evening. Would you call his room, please?"

"What's the name, sir?"

"Mr. Black," Jesus said. His flat tone told me Jesus was a little annoyed but he needed me to flash my cleavage so he didn't block my play.

Stanley tapped the keys on his computer. "I'm sorry, sir. I don't have a Mr. Black."

"I've played this game before," Jesus muttered. "Stanley, sorry I have to ask but can you keep a secret?"

"Assuredly, sir."

"Our friend is a tiny bit famous."

"Oh?"

The desk clerk was almost as intrigued by this news as he was with my tits.

"He's using an alias, I'm sure," Jesus said. "He's done it before. We've all done it but he changes up his aliases all the time to avoid fans."

"So you're saying Black is not his real name? Oh, dear."

"Yeah, you get it," I said.

"Well, we do host many celebrities at The Savoy. You can count on my discretion, I assure you."

"Try Mr. White," Jesus suggested.

Stanley perked up. "Ha-ha. Very good! Like in *Reservoir Dogs*!" Somehow, his big eyes got even wider. "Is it…him?"

"Him who?"

"Is it Mr. Tarantino? I wasn't working the desk this afternoon. The other clerk should have let me know — "

I placed one hand over one of Stanley's cold hands and put a finger to my lips. "Discretion, remember? If it were Quentin, he wouldn't want anyone to know."

Stanley nodded. "Of course. Where was I?"

"Looking up Mr. White," Jesus reminded him.

"No good. Wouldn't you know it? I have two Mr. Whites."

I jumped. "Do you have a Mr. Pink?"

"Uh…" *Tappity-tap-tap.* "Why, yes! Yes, we do!"

I couldn't resist rolling my eyes. "Of course, you do. Could you call his room, please?" I asked. "He wanted to choose the restaurant but I bet he didn't even make reservations. He's like that. You know the rich. They're geniuses with lots on their minds but they're like babies in the real world, too. They have to be coddled and babysat."

Stanley smirked. As a clerk at a major hotel, he probably knew the truth of my statement much better than I.

The clerk lifted the red phone at his elbow. I watched him stab out the room number on the keypad. This gambit wouldn't work in a newer hotel, but this was London. Even the new fancy hotels wanted to look like the old fancy hotels.

"I'm sorry. There's no answer."

"No problem," I said. "Thank you. We'll call him later. You have a great night."

"Thank you, madam. I certainly will."

Wanker, I thought. I loved British insults and witticisms. They're so right. Stanley would be thinking of me when he climbed into bed.

14

As we walked toward the elevator, Jesus looked at me in a new way. "How'd you know about the *Reservoir Dogs* alias thing?"

"Oh, c'mon. I've been around mob guys all my life. They didn't know how to act like mob guys until they watched *The Sopranos, Goodfellas* and everything Tarantino. How many times have you made me watch *Reservoir Dogs*? Like five times?"

"Only twice."

I sighed. "Felt like eight. Who knows how much of that is just lies that feed on themselves? If the movies had guys named Tad and Chad walking around beating people to death with tennis rackets, you'd all be walking around wearing pastel sweaters tied around your necks."

Jesus smirked. "And we'd all talk like we're from the rich parts of New Hampshire instead of from Jersey."

"Tragic. My dad thought gangsters should act and talk like any other people in business instead of getting caught up in the mythology."

"Your dad was smart. I watched a documentary about Owen Madden. He led the Irish mob in the way back. When he retired to

Arkansas, nobody knew he was the bootlegger who owned the Cotton Club. He lived totally under the radar. Smart. That's the way the business is going. For the Machine to survive, it's gotta be in big business, as legit as can be, at least mostly. Legit business pulls a lot of illegitimate shit so the distinction pretty much comes down to whether we carry guns or briefcases."

"Civilians wouldn't think so."

He shrugged.

"You watched a documentary about an old Irish gangster?"

"When you're recovering from gunshot wounds, you have a lot of free time to stare at Netflix."

I snorted. "We used to call the cops the Irish mob."

"Maybe one day we can get to a place where we aren't running from the good guys and the bad guys."

I looked him up and down. He still looked good but I thought I detected worry around his eyes. Or maybe he was tired. "Do you want to be a Normie, Jesus?" I cared about Jesus too much to be dishonest. I looked him in the eyes. "'Cuz if you think you can become a regular citizen, you are delusional."

"I've been working on that, but yeah, I know. Nobody leaves the Machine clean."

We took the elevator to the second floor. I guessed Luca wanted to be close to the exits.

He looked at me as if he was seeing an exotic bird for the first time. "Lily, you still want to get away from thug life, too, right? You're not getting a taste for it, are you? I've seen some guys go that way, in the Army and in the Machine. I don't want you to get like that."

"Take it easy, Jesus. You're not Batman and I'm not turning into the Joker."

"That hurts my feelings a little."

"Okay, you're a little bit Batman."

"You want to be Robin?"

"No. I'm not built to walk in anybody's shadow. It's cold in there."

"What do you want, Lily? Don't you want to feel safe? You and me, just regular civilians. No bullets and brains splattered every-where. Just…safe, y'know? With money, we could disappear like that old Irish gangster. It's possible, isn't it?"

"I'm a pretty Latina with a good rack, always underestimated. I've never felt safe in my life." Jesus was talking too much and I liked him a little less. I was more comfortable when he would only talk about movies.

"I didn't want to be a killer," I said. "Just because I don't get weepy about what I'm forced to do doesn't mean I'm a psycho."

"Okay."

"And as far as becoming a regular person goes, no, I don't want to be a Normie, either. Civilians are pushed around too much. Look around. They're living to pay down debt and die. They never get what they want because they're too busy scraping. They never get quite enough to have what they need."

The hallway was deserted so we stopped at the door of the man I killed. Jesus listened a full minute. It seemed like ages before he knocked on the door. "Room service!"

Dead men don't answer the door. They apparently don't have backup staying with them, either.

Jesus produced the key card from his back pocket. It was smeared with blood. "What's the other choice?"

"Huh?"

"You don't want to be a PTA mom who gets pushed around and goes into a panic trying to figure out how to pay a bill. You don't want to be a killer outlaw. What's the other choice?"

"Freedom."

"Free *costs*, Lily. It costs a lot. So far, the tally is a lot of blood." Jesus pulled his SIG from the belt holster in the small of his back and opened the door.

I flicked the light on with the muzzle of Lonnie's .38. A naked dead woman lay sprawled on the bed. It was the girl who lived in the flat below mine.

"Denise!"

Jesus was right. The cost of living free is too high. This death was on me. It was the first death that made me weep.

15

I didn't want to, but I looked closer. Denise's eyes were open, staring into forever, but there was no shine there. No one was home. Her skin was waxy and yellowish. The belt with which my downstairs neighbor was strangled was still around her throat, twisted like a tourniquet.

"Don't touch anything." Jesus checked the bathroom. Besides my dead neighbor, we were alone.

"There's a nice big bathtub in there," he said. "Why he wouldn't kill her there instead of in the bed is beyond me. Idiot."

"Just as dead, either way."

Jesus scanned the murder scene with a trained and experienced eye. "There's blood under her fingernails. She put up a fight."

"For all the good it did her." I wrinkled my nose when the stench hit me. She had soiled herself.

"This is a crime scene. If you're going to throw up, don't do it here."

I gave Jesus a withering look. "Do I look like I'm about to lose my shit?" I look down at the brown sheets and the wetness soaking into the mattress. "Poor choice of words."

"On the plus side," Jesus said, "you already killed her killer."

"Why did Luca do this? If he was going to keep tabs on me, why didn't he just kill Denise in her apartment and be done with it?"

"I can think of a dozen reasons," Jesus said. "Maybe Luca wanted to get close. He probably planned to take over the apartment below you and bug your place. Denny's top priority isn't killing you. He wants the money back."

"He certainly does want me dead — "

"He wants the money first. That's why you aren't dead already. I should have known he wouldn't wait for me to recover fully before he sent out more operators. He's worried you'd spend all the skim before I got my stitches out."

"More operators? Cherry, Luca, and the guys at the mansion. How many more would he send?"

"As many as it takes, I guess." Jesus sat in a chair and watched me while I wept over Denise. When I was done, he said, "Lily. Look at me."

"Jesus, don't try that Chili Palmer shit on me."

"How much was in those suitcases, Lily?"

"What?"

"You heard me. How much money makes all this worth it?"

I looked at Denise. She was pushed around all her short life. Now she was dead because I wanted to be free. "No amount of money makes this worth it. I didn't know her that well. It's not like we were besties. At first, I thought she wanted a friend to be her amateur psychiatrist. I was going to tell her that if she can't afford a shrink's rates, maybe she could call one of those psychic hotlines. After we talked a while, I figured out she wasn't really needy or neurotic. Denise was just trying to get out from under. I liked her for that. When she made a pass at me, it wasn't desperate or sad. I feel bad for making a joke out of it earlier. Denise was nice. I haven't met many people who are nice."

"She was a civilian caught in the crossfire, so I have to ask you again, how *much*, Lily?"

"One-point-seven."

"Million?"

"What do you think I meant? Yen? Pesos?"

"How much is left?"

"Plenty."

"How much is plenty?"

"It doesn't matter."

"Of course it matters."

"Denny wants me dead either way. Nobody steals from the Machine and get away clean. Maybe I wouldn't have this problem if you'd killed Denny in the first place."

"Denny was like a brother to me and he did save me in L.A. I would have bled out if not for him."

"You're only alive because he needed you to track me down. Maybe Luca was following you all this time. When you missed me in Madrid, maybe you should have taken off for the South Pole or something. If you had, maybe Denise would be alive. Maybe we're both safer if we're on opposite sides of the planet."

"That's a lot of maybes. If I hadn't come to find you, someone else would have. And never seeing you again would have killed me."

"Not in the same way I killed Denise."

"Not for nothing but also, if I didn't find you, Denny would kill me."

We stared at the corpse in the bed for a long time. I wondered if we were looking into our future.

16

"You got a time machine on you, Jesus?"

He made a show of patting down his pockets and shook his head.

"Then let's stop talking about what's done and focus on the to-do list. What do we do now?"

"When Denny sent me, he was hoping I could talk some sense into you — "

He caught my hard look and smiled. "What can I tell you, baby? More flies with honey. I had hoped I could work a deal so Denny gets whatever's left of the skim and I tell him you're dead."

"Come up with another plan. How do you feel about killing Denny now?"

"Not much better. Kill him and he'll be replaced by somebody else who wants the money back. That's a lot of money. The Machine isn't going to write it off. Panama Bob must have been skimming for years to have that much socked away. If he wanted to get away with it, he should have settled for much less and disappeared without being so greedy."

"I lost my dad to the Machine, Jesus. He was killed in front of me. I am owed. The skim isn't just my escape clause. It's my compensation."

"I get it. Denny's not getting his money back. I'm not going to try to convince you —"

"It's not just about the money, Jesus. Bob had more than money in those suitcases. He had an insurance policy in there."

"What?"

"He was a smart guy, smarter than anyone gave him credit for, anyway. I think he planned to take the money with him into the Witness Protection Program."

"How could you know that?"

"Because when I got the money out of the suitcases, there was more than money in there. I found a memory stick. I opened it as soon as I got out of New York. It's plenty of evidence for the feds."

"Evidence of what?"

"Names, numbers, events, dates, times. He knew who paid what to whom and who got killed because they didn't pay. Panama Bob had the whole hierarchy of the Machine mapped out. There's spreadsheets in there: weapons deals, drug deals, addresses, shipping dates, drops, payouts, bribes paid. It's the whole organization on a silver platter. He was ready to rat out everybody if he didn't get away clean."

"Holy shit. Bob was a rat on top of a thief? I did not see that coming."

"Nobody sees the rat coming," I said. "Mom always said they're sneaky creatures. Everything seems cool and clean and then suddenly they show up in your house and inside your cereal box."

"There's no statute of limitations on murder. That memory stick could burn it all down. Vincent Lima's Machine was heavily damaged when we left New York. With Denny as boss, they've recovered but that information could erase it forever. Where is this memory stick now?"

"In a safety deposit box in Miami. They get that, the feds bust the whole operation wide open. Panama Bob recorded everything going back years."

"Yeah, he was like a little girl that way," Jesus said. "Dear Diary, guess who killed who and who's running numbers in Bed-Stuy today? When I threw Bob off the side of a building, I thought he was a dummy who gambled too much and skimmed too much off the top. I had no idea he was a crazy rat, too."

"Surprise, surprise, and get over it. The stakes just went up. You and Big Denny and every job you ever did for the Machine is on that memory stick."

"This just gets better and better. You could have gone to the feds and gotten immunity, taken the skim into the Witness Protection Program — "

"No, I couldn't. You're in the rat files. I couldn't do that to you, Jesus."

"So I owe Denny and I owe you," Jesus replied. "You don't have to spell it out, Lily, and you don't have to tally the bill. You know I still love you."

The guys in the Machine used to call me the Ice Queen. I was that, but the look on Jesus' face made me melt a little. I smiled. "Jesus loves, understands and forgives."

"I do."

It would have been great to be able to forgive myself. I couldn't, though. Denise wasn't my enemy. Her death didn't make me a winner. People tell themselves stories about this or that shitty thing they did in the past. They let some things go and maybe they should. When the mistake is something you can't repair, you shouldn't let yourself off the hook so easily. If I forgave myself for Denise's death, I would be a monster.

I could let the rest go but Denise's death was one I had to carry. Somebody had to pay and I chose Big Denny De Molina.

17

I reached for the duvet to cover Denise's face, but Jesus stopped me as he pulled on gloves. "Careful what you touch. If they somehow connect the forensics to Luca, I'm fine with that. I'd forgotten how much of a dick that guy was."

I couldn't take Denise's vacant stare much longer. "Let's go."

"Not yet. Luca was sent to find you, but maybe you're right. Maybe he was following me. Let's make sure he didn't leave anything behind that will connect me with him...at least until we can get out of the country."

I looked in the bathroom so I didn't have to be around Denise's body. Luca had entered the country very recently. His toiletries were all brand new, bought here in London. There was no way the killer got through airport security with big bottles of mouthwash and shampoo.

When I returned, Jesus had taken the drawers out of the desk and the dresser. He looked as disappointed as the kid who comes up with zip at an Easter egg hunt. "I don't like finding nothing. When you find nothing, you never know if there was nothing to find."

"Did you look under the mattress?" I ask.

"First thing."

I didn't know where else to look. I did a slow circle, wondering where I'd hide something if I were Luca. Jesus checked under a lamp and then under the shade. "You looked under the bed, right?"

"When we came in. Buddy of mine in the MPs got shot in the ankle for being careless that way."

"You want to start ripping up carpet?"

"Nah. We don't know what we're looking for. Might be something that doesn't exist. Besides, it would have to be somewhere unobtrusive but accessible." Even as he said it, Jesus looked distracted. I followed his gaze to an air vent.

Jesus looked at me and smiled. "On three, tell me what movie this reminds you of. One, two, three — "

He said, "*Grosse Pointe Blank!*"

"*No Country for Old Men!*" I said.

In both movies, somebody hides something in a hotel air vent. Jesus conceded that *No Country for Old Men* was brilliant, but I could tell he was a little disappointed that we didn't chorus his choice in stereo. While I reached for coins to twist the screw, Jesus pulled out a multi-tool. He had a screwdriver attachment that fit.

His mood lightened as he unscrewed the vent cover. "Congratulations, Ms. Vasquez. It's a boy." He pulled out a wallet and two passports. One passport was Canadian, the other American. Both picture IDs were of Luca. I hadn't had a good look at the man I'd killed until I stared into those pictures. He looked like anybody else. There was nothing especially terrifying or evil about his eyes, no clue that he could be capable of strangling Denise in his hotel bed.

Jesus pulled a piece of paper from the wallet and showed it to me like I should know what it meant. It had what looked like a scrawled telephone number written on it.

"Denny had me memorize this same number," Jesus said. "It's the handyman's burner phone."

"The handyman?"

"A man who's handy. Sometimes he's a woman."

"Meaning?"

"Tech support. When we're working for the Machine, we need locals for the little problems that crop up. Having a handyman on call is one of the things I missed when I was freelancing. It's good to have a number to call when you need supplies or a car or...anything really. The Machine is like Buddha. The Machine provides. I took the handyman's recommendation for a place to stay. That's how I ended up in the same hotel as Luca."

"That's where you got your SIG, too, isn't it?"

"Sure. The one on me isn't my original. I lost my first pistol in Hollywood when I got shot."

"You loved that gun."

"Yeah, well, I was distracted by all the blood spurting out of me at the time."

"You know what I think, Jesus?"

"Tell me."

"I think Luca killed Denise here but I bet he planned to put the body in your room before he left."

"That would be awkward."

"The handyman told you and Luca to stay in the same hotel and you don't think Denny was setting you up for more trouble after you got the skim from me?"

"Shit," Jesus said.

"We're surrounded by a lake of it, yeah."

18

"How does this handyman thing work exactly?"

"You know all those container ships carrying stuff back and forth across the ocean? Very little of it is actually checked by anyone. It's too much. No Customs officer is enthusiastic about digging around the back of a container full of somebody's living room furniture."

"There's more than change in those couch cushions? I didn't see that in the spreadsheets, but I didn't spend a whole lot of time looking at the evidence on that memory stick, either."

"The Machine was dealt a blow when we left New York but they've been expanding since."

"Denny got plans for world domination?"

"Guess so. He's connected. I recovered from my wounds in Mexico."

"Denny couldn't stick to a diet, but he's trying to take over the world?"

Jesus smirked. "It's not like the Machine has a handyman in every city, but people know people. Connections get made when contraband and money changes hands. Usually, equipment comes from some guy who knows some guy in prison and the word gets around somehow. Nothing on the grid and nothing on the net. Then there's the black markets. Once in a while, you'll hear about a drug bust or some weapons sting and the cops will crow about how they got a kilo of coke or seized a few guns. That's a teacup out of an ocean. It's not even missed."

I knew what Jesus meant. Wherever I'd traveled, I'd been alert to what goes on below the surface. In the daytime, every city had its first-date face on for the regular citizens and the tourists. There's always a different face beneath the makeup. The dark side comes out to play at night.

"How'd it work with your handyman, exactly?" I asked.

"I called the handyman. He played fetch. Anybody can get a gun within a day. If you didn't have a handyman, how would you get your weapons?" Jesus asked. "Come to think of it, how did you get your weapon?"

"The old fashioned way. I stole it."

"How?"

"Every city has a cop bar. I followed one home. The first time it didn't work. This is England. They aren't gun crazy like back home. If I did the same thing back home, I could have had my pick of a bunch of weapons from an arsenal."

"True."

"I found a cop who lived alone and waited for him to go to work. Then I went to the back door looking for a key under a flowerpot."

"That's my trick!" Jesus exclaimed.

"Your trick didn't work. There was no key, but it was easy to convince a landlady that I was a one-night stand coming back for my earrings."

"Smooth," he said. "Let's go."

"Search over?"

"We've already been here way too long. Nothing more for us except to get out, call the handyman and get you a fresh passport."

"I'm not going to Finland."

"How about Denmark? The happiest people in the world live in Denmark."

A knock at the door made us freeze.

The knock came again, harder. "Room service!"

We pulled our guns. "Calling out 'room service,' is my trick, too," Jesus whispered. He pointed his SIG ready to blast through the door.

"I'll look through the peephole," I suggested.

"As soon as the peephole darkens, they'll shoot you through the eye," Jesus said.

"How do you know?"

"Because that's what I'd do."

"What do you want?" I called out.

"Compliments of the hotel, madam."

I recognized that voice. It was the front desk clerk. Stanley was probably hoping to get an autograph and a selfie with Quentin Tarantino.

"We are pleased to have you — "

"Leave it!" I yelled. "We're fucking!"

The guy on the other side of the door didn't seem to move right away.

Jesus gave me a wink and whispered, "Do your Meg Ryan."

I glared back. "Really?"

"Please?"

"I told you I'd never do that again."

"Don't kink-shame me, angel."

I took a deep breath and did my version of the diner scene from *When Harry Met Sally.* "Give it to me, Q! Give it to me! I'm begging you! *Uh! Uh! Uh!* Yeah, baby! That's so good!"

Jesus pounded the headboard with his fist with an increasing tempo.

"Please! I can't take much more! Harder! Harder! Oh, Gawd! You're killing me! Yes! Yes! Yes!"

"I swear to God," Jesus yelled, "if that room service guy is still out there when I'm done, I'll fuck him next! Put your toes in my mouth!"

Stanley scurried away. We heard his footfalls down the corridor and the ding of the elevator.

When we opened the door, the hallway was empty except for a cart that held a plate of caviar and a bottle of champagne. A note on stationery rimmed with gold foil read:

Welcome to The Savoy, Mr. Pink. We're pleased to host such a distinguished guest and hope you'll make our hotel your home whenever you visit our city. You can always count on our discretion. Please let us know what we can do to make your stay most enjoyable, sir.

I stared at it. "Stanley signed it himself and added his private phone number."

Jesus glanced at the note. "Goddammit, Quentin is going to get a weird phone call. When Scotland Yard talks to the staff, Stanley will tell them he heard Quentin Tarantino fucking this poor girl to death. It might take them a while to sort out that Luca is the killer."

"Jesus, that's not going to be — "

"Yeah, yeah, I know. It will work out, but Quentin — "

"Jesus loves him, this I know." I gave my ex the heavy sigh and stink eye. "Do you need a moment to get your priorities rearranged?"

Caviar tastes like salty slime. I left that crap but took champagne. When we got a moment, I planned to cry over Denise some more with a little bit of liquid solace.

We didn't spend long in Jesus' room. He changed his clothes and grabbed his stuff. We exited the hotel out the back without paying his bill. We had a handyman to meet and a country to get the fuck out of before we could do any more damage to England. Or to Quentin Tarantino's reputation.

W e headed straight for the handyman's house. It was a basement flat in Tottenham. The city street where the cab dropped us off looked like a third world country, not England. I felt like we were being watched and told Jesus so.

He nodded. "Probably. That feeling you get at the back of your neck that eyes are on you is the only evidence that mental telepathy could be real. They've done studies. Spider sense is a real thing."

"Maybe what's real is that I know a bad neighborhood when I see one. We're carrying bags and dressed too well. Street smarts is what's real."

We made our way around to the back of the apartment building. Three young toughs sat at the rear entrance smoking. I doubted they were more than eighteen years old. Two young men with thin blond hair flanked a large bald man in a sleeveless leather jacket covered in silver buckles. Both blonds whispered to the guy in the middle. He nodded and pushed them away. Then he smiled at me, not in a friendly way.

The alpha thought he was so bad, he had to advertise. Barbell piercings shot through both his eyebrows haphazardly. His wiry arms were a riot of tattoos and he sported a barcode tattoo across his fore-head. His forehead was so prominent, I thought of a beluga whale. He looked me over a little too long before addressing Jesus. "Our returning champion! Nice suit! All in black, huh? Late for a funeral, are we?"

"Somebody's funeral, yeah," Jesus replied.

"You're the Yank who were here just the other day. The lads tell me you didn't pay the toll when you were here last."

Jesus didn't blink. "I'm here for Reilly."

"Got an appointment?" one of the blonds asked.

The leader looked back at the new comedian and told him to shut the fuck up. Satisfied the junior gang member was cowed, he turned back to Jesus. "Your lady is a right bird. Maybe she could pay the toll for you. She'd have to pay twice, but she might have a fun time doing — "

"You don't want to mess with her," Jesus said. "She bites."

"Well, that's a shame." He put his hands in his pockets, shrugged and smiled wide. "Reilly's not available at the moment. Would you care to leave a message?"

The pair backing his play caught his drift. They stood in front of the door to the building and tried to look bigger than they were, shoulders high, chests puffed out.

Jesus glanced up and then stared. "Oh, my god! Why is Reilly on the damn roof? Reilly! Don't jump! Don't jump!"

I looked up and the leader did, too. I caught the movement out of the corner of my eye as Jesus punched the tattooed man in his exposed throat. As the bad guy went down, the other two pulled switchblades.

They were too late. I'd already pulled Luca's sawed-off from under my coat and pointed it at them. They stood so close together, I could have shot them both in the crotch by moving the muzzle back and forth just a few inches.

As the tattooed thug choked and struggled to breathe, the pair of toughs shrank back, not so tough anymore. They moved to go, but I stopped them. "Leave the blades."

Jesus gave me a look that said to leave well enough alone but I wanted those knives. The kids dropped their weapons. I told them to go start a lemonade stand and they took off.

I tried to imagine Tottenham's tough guy without all the bad tattoos and attitude. Nothing against tattoos, I have a couple myself. However, mine don't look like they were inked with a ballpoint pen in jail.

The fallen man was beginning to get his breath back. He sneered up at me and croaked, "W-what?"

Pointing the muzzle of the shotgun in his blue eyes, I told him, "You didn't pay the toll." Then I kicked him in the teeth with the point of my boot.

I bent to collect the knives as Jesus searched the crying tattooed guy. His front teeth were knocked loose. Maybe his jaw was broken, too. Jesus took a switchblade from the thug as well as his wallet.

As we did this, an elderly couple stepped out of the door to the apartment building. The world had trained them. They looked away and pretended they didn't see a Latin couple with weapons standing over a crying man. The thug no doubt terrorized them from time to time when they left their flat, so they owed him nothing. The old man and woman hurried away.

Jesus looked down at the injured man and pointed at me. "If she ever sees you again, she'll kill you. Do you doubt it?"

The tattooed thug eyed me a moment before looking away. He shook his head.

"Then go home and apologize to your mother, clean up your room and make your bed. I've got your wallet. I know where you live. I'll be around to check up on you. It will be a surprise inspection. If your bed isn't made during daylight hours or if I find socks on the floor, I'll call this 'right bird,' and she'll kick you to death. Do you doubt me?"

He shook his head again. Jesus helped him to his feet and pushed him in the same direction that his crew fled. He disappeared around a corner.

"Neat trick," I said. "You use that a lot?"

"Just fucking with him. As soon as you have somebody's home address, they're fucked. Must be the old cop in me."

"No, I mean the look-at-the-roof trick was cool."

"Worked on me once in Basic. You never forget a lesson like that. When they look up, *bam!*"

"Nice."

"Except it wasn't a throat punch. A guy kicked me in the balls."

"What did you do to the guy who taught you that lesson?"

Jesus smiled at the memory. "About a month after we were on our first tour, he thought I had let it go, I did something similar. Every magician knows the value of misdirection."

"What'd you do?"

"I pointed at the ground and told him he dropped his pocket."

"What? *That* worked?"

"It's a kid joke but, with conviction, you can sell anything and get anyone to look where you want. Just stare at the ground and point. I cracked him upside the head as he looked down. It only takes a second of inattention."

"How did that feel?"

"He probably still gets headaches. I pistol whipped him, but just the once. Finished with a kick to the balls for good measure."

"I mean how was it for you? How did getting vengeance feel?"

I could tell he didn't want to talk about it. "You've got blood on the toe of your boot, Lily. Maybe it felt like you do now."

"I do feel pretty great, all things considered," I said. "After the shock of finding Denise, that was very therapeutic. I needed to kick something, so thank you."

Jesus sighed. I sensed he was disappointed in me. He expected me to be better than he was. I had no idea why.

"Let's go meet Reilly," I said.

J esus knocked on the handyman's door. No answer came.

"Maybe nobody's home," I suggested.

"A guy like Reilly has got no place to be besides here."
Jesus knocked harder.

"Maybe he's dead, like the last door we knocked on — "

The door popped open and a man with long gray hair hanging in his face stared at us. "You want to see the wizard? Nobody sees the wizard!"

He tried to slam the door but Jesus shoved his Tanino Crisci shoe in the way and pushed his way in. "Hello again, Reilly. Don't be rude. I'm here on business."

"Didn't expect to see you so soon. Nobody told me you were coming."

"Did they tell you to expect me to show up dead?"

Reilly said nothing to that.

The apartment was dark. The peeling paint on the beige walls revealed gray spots underneath. The flat had a musty smell that competed with the stench of body odor. If I had to live like this, I'd shoot myself in the head within a month.

Unscraped dishes caked with burnt food had been piled in the sink and forgotten. The only thing I could see that looked like it cost more than fifty bucks was the big plasma screen. Beneath that, a PS4 sat on the floor. Reilly had been playing *Far Cry 4*. The game was paused. I'd been wanting to play that, but I'm more of a PC gamer than a console player and I'd been deep into *Just Cause 3* lately. I missed my computer already.

"I didn't get the call," Reilly complained. "I'm supposed to get a call first. And who's she?"

"I needed to make sure you didn't call anyone else before we paid a visit."

"Call who?"

"You deal with a lot of shady characters, Reilly."

"I know some villains, sure."

"You dealt with Luca? Got him some gear, right?"

"Not paid to remember names. I'm paid to forget them."

I pulled the sawed-off out and pointed it at Reilly's head. "Recognize this? Did you give this shotgun to a guy named Luca?"

Jesus waved me off. "Easy, now. This is not that sort of visit."

I put the shotgun down and stared at the handyman. He seemed more scared of me than of Jesus. I was the wildcard he didn't know. I sat in an old green chair. I practiced my best hostile glare as I dug one of my new switchblades into the arm of the chair, stabbing the fabric repeatedly and doing crazy eyes for full effect.

"Did you get a call from New York since I left?" Jesus asked.

"No."

"Big Denny De Molina didn't call you?"

"Nah."

"None of his people called you?"

"I said no, didn't I?"

"Good. I believe you. She doesn't, but I do. Keep your eyes on me and try not to worry about her. As long as I believe you, you're probably safe. The moment I think you're screwing me over, I let her loose on you with that blade. Understand?"

The handyman nodded and stole glances at me. He wasn't looking at me furtively the same way Stanley did back at The Savoy.

He was not ogling. Reilly was frightened and needed to know how much space there was between us at all times.

I smiled. "Picture yourself at the zoo, Reilly. The zoo is nice, but the lions are out of the cage and it might be feeding time. Understand?"

This was a nice change of pace. Acting badass was changing my relationship with half my species. As Reilly looked into my eyes, I stabbed the blade into the arm of the chair again. It's easy to act crazy. All you have to do is stare and think of all the terrible things you've seen, like Denise strangled in a hotel bed for no good reason. Come to think of it, maybe I didn't have to act crazy. Maybe I was sort of crazy. Maybe I am.

Reilly asked Jesus what he could get him. He wasn't offering a drink.

"She needs a passport."

"Will she stop ruining my upholstery if I do?"

"She'll do to you what she's doing to that chair if you don't."

The handyman was handy. We stayed with him for a day and a night. Reilly wanted us to leave and come back but we couldn't risk that. By the time we got to Heathrow, our weapons were wiped clean and deposited in as many pieces as we could manage, trash bins mostly.

Jesus told me not to watch TV but I did, anyway. That's how I knew the bodies of Luca, Cherry and Denise had all been found. There was still a lot of excitement over the mass murder and arson in Camberley, of course. So far, the police hadn't leaked anything about how Quentin Tarantino could possibly be involved. (Sorry for any inconvenience, Q. We are fans.)

Reilly set me up with a Canadian passport. We weren't headed to Finland so that was some consolation.

I'd known married couples that wouldn't cheat on each other unless they were visiting another country. For instance, I received three offers of sex with married men in Madrid. (What the fuck, Madrid?) Anyway, I had a new rule. If I committed mass murder outside of the US, it didn't count. Too bad the authorities didn't agree.

Getting on the plane, I resolved to start fresh...except for Denise. That shit would not rub out no matter how hard I scrubbed. I loved London so much, but I could never go back. London had too many ghosts.

Weaponless, we flew to Miami International Airport. Plenty of ghosts waited in Florida, too, but those specters were all from Jesus' tortured past.

I knew a guy in Manalapan. I was sure we could hide out with him until we figured our next play. My friend had a house by the beach, a pool and a hot tub. Hiding out from Denny while retrieving the memory stick wasn't going to be comfortable. As long as I'd known him, Jesus wore black Armani suits. He wouldn't care for Florida's heat.

Arriving in Florida, I was worried about more than the weather and Big Denny's assassins searching for us. Jesus was my first serious boyfriend. The guy in Manalapan had been my second.

Dealing with the TSA at Miami International wasn't much more than the usual ordeal. The agent asked what I did for a living. I told him I was an art student. Technically, that much was true. So far, murdering people to survive was just a hobby.

The TSA guy then asked how long I intended to stay. I replied that I was a Canadian returning from a tour of museums in London. I explained that my parents were snowbirds who owned a condo in Boca. I flirted a little, mentioning that all I wanted to do was lie on a beach and work on my tan before returning home to Toronto in a week.

Jesus got pulled out of line and patted down. The TSA didn't like his look. They went through his luggage and asked a lot of questions. His passport told them he was a US citizen, but the name was different and, as far as they knew, he was selling Japanese toys. The sales pamphlets in his suitcase were the clincher.

Once we got through security, I asked Jesus what he knew about Japanese toys.

"I know how to pronounce the words Japanese and toys," he said.

"Where'd you get the brochures?"

"The handyman. I assume the sales brochures and this suitcase were stolen from a salesman and repurposed."

"I didn't like Reilly but having a handyman on call is kind of like — "

"Alfred to Batman."

"Oh, stop."

"JARVIS to Ironman?"

"Grow up, Jesus."

"If we wanted to grow up, we wouldn't be who we are."

I thought about that for a moment. I wondered how long this ride could last before we were dead or in jail. Or dead in jail. If the Machine had connections on other continents, it was certain they could reach into any prison population to murder us.

The outlook for our life expectancy was not rosy. Even as I pushed that thought away, I was aware that I was pretending my grisly demise was a far-off problem. Living the way I did, running from bad men, I didn't feel young. Thug life ages a person. At this rate, Jesus and I were already far beyond middle age. Old people talk about their twilight years. It was a good bet I was in my twilight month.

When I was eighteen, one of my father's work associates expired young. Dad said his friend had died of "inconvenient gunshot wounds." We went to the funeral. The casket was not closed but it should have been. I saw the corpse. The funeral technicians had tried to fix up the gunshot victim. His face was like a waxy ill-fitting mask.

"These things rarely happen willy-nilly. When they shoot you in the face," Dad told me, "it's an extra insult, like a fuck you to the family trying to bury their kid with dignity. Better to have a beautiful, framed picture on the casket and leave it at that.

"When they shoot you in the mouth," Dad continued, "that means you were a rat and deserved to die."

"Sounds kind of elaborate," I said. "Don't people just shoot at each other?"

"Shootouts only happen when there's so much disorder that we have to go to war. Otherwise, when somebody gets clipped, you go for a ride in a car and you don't come back. There's no back and forth. We aren't in the cowboy business. It's not about being a quick draw. When it happens, the button man will probably be a buddy, somebody the rat trusts."

There was much more meaning to the geography of gunshot wounds. If shot in the belly, someone probably wanted information out of the guy before he bled out. Belly wounds are the most painful and a slower way to go. Get your dingus shot off? He was sleeping with somebody's wife.

"A man can live without a dingus," Dad joked. "Plus he gets the added benefit of a lesson learned. He sure won't make that mistake again."

Dad explained all this to me during the funeral from the second pew behind the widow. I figured out later that my father wasn't just talking to me. He didn't mind if the crying widow overheard his lecture. He wanted her to know he wasn't a friend of the deceased. He ordered the hit.

"Sometimes you see a guy with a lot of holes, more than Swiss cheese and bloodier. That's usually not anger. That's panic. It tells you whoever did the hit, musta been his first time. He's probably not cut out to be a button man. On the other hand, two in the head and one in the heart? That's just business. Nothing personal, but a pro hit. Most times a guy gets shot? He's on his knees at the edge of the grave he dug. He knows he did something wrong, something he can't come back from. Most guys who need to disappear, just disappear."

Since going on the run from Big Denny De Molina, I understood my father better. There are two worlds. Regular people with regular jobs hope for one vacation a year. They spend time with their families when they can. They're just trying to pay bills and taxes. They just want to eat and get by. If they can avoid car accidents, cancer and heart disease, life for civilians can be relatively safe for quite some time.

My dad's world was full of secrets and ambition and danger, a world where patterns of gunshot wounds conveyed meaning.

People misunderstand something about life in the mob. It's not as crazy as it seems. There are rules because the enterprise is really about making money. The violence is not the disorder or an end in itself. Slayings are the attempt to stop chaos, to keep Mob World and Regular World separate.

J esus and I stepped out into the Florida sunshine. Miami always seems the same, like the city picked a hot summer in the late fifties and decided to stick with it.

Miami has a party reputation: young people, all splashy dresses and tattoos. The smell of suntan lotion substitutes for perfume and cologne. That's the tourism commercial. It's not the real Miami.

Floridians here may not all look the same, but they are variations on a theme. The old people all dress in shades of white and move slowly on unsteady feet. The older white people who live here look craggy and freckled from the sun, their skin ready to burst forth with suspicious moles at any moment. They wear oversized sunglasses and mutter to each other in a way that makes every conversation look confidential. The tourists crawling back to the airport and headed for Departures are all as red as boiled lobsters.

Jesus surveyed the crowd, looking for enemies. Finding none, he told me he required one pulled pork sandwich. After that, he needed to make a phone call.

"Pulled pork?"

"I never had them when I was here before," he admitted. "On *Dexter*, he made them sound good."

"That TV show about a serial killer in Miami? Never watched it."

"I liked that character."

"Gee, it sure is a mystery why, huh?"

Jesus shrugged. "He was righteous ... mostly. They really messed up the ending of that show — "

"Do you ever do anything besides go to movies and watch TV?"

"Sure. Right now I'm working on a mission to save the life of the love of my life."

I let that pass and asked about the phone call. "Calling another handyman?"

"Something like that. I know a guy. I need to see if he can help, maybe get us out of this mess."

"Out? Like transport us to another planet where there is no Machine?"

"Interplanetary travel is just about what it might take, yeah," he said.

It was Sunday so I couldn't retrieve the memory stick from the safety deposit box. All that scary data on the Machine would have to wait.

We rented a family van that wouldn't attract attention. I took the wheel and steered east. Even though there was an ocean between me and the carnage in London and Camberley, I didn't begin to relax until we'd blended in, anonymous amid the flow of traffic.

We headed north, up the coast. As we passed a state trooper, my heartbeat kicked up a notch. I wondered if Interpol had pulled my face from a surveillance camera somewhere. London is peppered with so many security cameras, the risk was significant. Jesus told me not to worry about it. "Between your sunglasses and your wig, you could be a lot of people."

"Even with all that gear they have to surveil us?"

"You're fine. They've got too much data to mine to pick you out of a crowd — "

"Said the guy who is so paranoid about being in an airport, you walked around with a limp, all bent over."

"They could have my regular walk in a biometric file."

I didn't know whether to take him seriously or not. "You got through TSA without getting arrested."

"TSA guys aren't trained detectives, they aren't paid enough. They may as well be the guy behind the counter at a bodega who yells at anybody who takes too long deciding to buy a magazine."

"You were pretty cool back there, considering who is looking for you. The FBI has been looking for you for a long time. Didn't you consider not coming back?"

"And leave you hangin'? I couldn't do that. Besides, I had my ID and a good story."

"And your sales pamphlets."

"Yeah, and my sales pamphlets. Airport security used to scare me more. Now, I know the trick. They're looking at everybody so they've got too much to look at to spot a pro. They've built a haystack out of needles and it's so big, they can't find any particular needle. Do you know how many people are on the Do Not Fly list, including yours truly?"

I shrugged.

"The official number is: Way too many to keep track of. New identity, new license to fly."

I glanced in the rear view mirror looking for pursuers and hoped he wasn't just saying all this to placate me.

"As long as you look compliant, you're fine," he said. "Look tired instead of terrified. Yawn a lot and it'll make them yawn, too. That calms them down."

"That works?"

"It's called mirroring. You adopt someone else's posture and they feel less threatened. A guy who's trying to blow up a plane doesn't yawn. He sweats. That's the sort of thing that any idiot can pick up on. You don't have to be Sherlock Holmes to catch a sweaty guy whose hands are shaking. People who are about to kill themselves and others sweat through their clothes. That's why the air conditioning is cranked up so high in airports. They want you cold.

If you've got any dark deeds in mind, you'll stand out in the crowd."

The more Jesus talked, the more I began to relax. I forced myself to watch the road ahead instead of obsessing about the road behind us.

"Most TSA agents don't want a hassle any more than anyone else," Jesus continued. "If they figure you're ready to eat shit so you don't miss your flight, they're generally satisfied. Bow your head and they figure you're under control. I'd never travel through Israel, though. Those guys are all former Mossad. Protecting El A`l is serious biz. Those are detectives who know what they're doing and they don't fuck around. Leave a bag unattended at an airport in the States and they'll shut down the airport for hours. Leave a bag unattended for a minute in Israel, they'll blow up your underwear in a heartbeat. Blow up a building in Israel and they're rebuilding it overnight because they don't want to give the bombers the satisfaction. They've got their shit locked down."

"Our airport security is that fucked up?"

"Sure. They're low-wage folks who are exhausted and working double shifts to pay for their kids' braces. They're mostly just trying to keep the lines moving. Occasionally, they'll escalate situations because they're new or maybe they're bored or feeling powerless or sad. Some misguided folks in airport security probably think that if they make the process more unpleasant for everybody, they'll scare up a bomber. Instead, they make everybody nervous and cranky so the sweaty guy is harder to spot."

"You've convinced me, Jesus. I never want to fly again."

"That's disappointing," Jesus said. "After we sort out this business, I was thinking you and I should disappear to French Polynesia."

"Not Finland?"

"I've seen pictures. In Polynesia, the water's so blue it looks fake."

I didn't want to speculate on what might happen between us if we could get the Machine off our backs. Not yet, anyway. Relief didn't seem remotely possible so I didn't want to tease myself. I tried to keep Jesus off that subject. "From what you say, it's not safe to fly anywhere — "

"Safe is for civilians. Safe is for staying home and doing nothing. It's actually much safer to fly than it used to be, especially since they put nine-dollar locks on cockpit doors."

"You just made clear the TSA isn't stopping anybody."

"Hijackers aren't stopped by airport security, no. Terrorists are stopped in one of two ways. Once in a while, bad guys get jacked by intelligence that gets picked up nowhere near the airport. Old-fashioned police work is what makes the FBI scary. Used to be, agents couldn't find their asses with both hands. The FBI has stepped up its game a bit."

"What's the other way hijackers get caught?"

"The passengers swarm them, beat the shit out of them with their shoes and try to keep themselves from killing the hijacker before landing. Airline *passengers* have stepped up their game since 9/11. But, you know...if you're freaked out about flying now, we could take a slow boat and enjoy the cruise. Or buy a boat and disappear into the Caribbean."

For the first time since we left Miami International, I dared to slide a glance his way. He looked serious.

"Let me try to make peace with Denny, Lily. We can't get off the planet, but if I can work out something with him, maybe we won't have to learn how to speak Martian."

"You're dreaming."

"I'm dreaming of you in a bikini in the sunshine and safe."

"You said safety was for civilians."

"Maybe we could become civilians. The memory stick would sink the Machine. Denny would be smart to take that instead of the money. We could be on that boat sailing for the Dominican soon."

"I thought you hated boats and swimming."

"I do, but for you, I'll wear a life vest."

We hadn't eaten since the flight so I pulled off the highway to find a restaurant in Boca. Jesus picked a joint from the GPS. The small parking lot was empty except for one car and we had the restaurant to ourselves. Everything in the place was red: the booths, the waiter's vest and the plates. Only one waiter was on duty and violins and cellos sighed at each other in the background. The restaurant's decor was what you'd get if Valentine's Day threw up.

I'd come for the air conditioning and to relax in the plush seats. This felt like the first moment since our reunion that we could stop and breathe a little deeper. Jesus cared less for the pork sandwich than he'd hoped, but he told me loved the view. We were in a dark booth tucked away at the back. I was the view.

"If you don't like the pork sandwich, don't finish it. Order something else."

Jesus shook his head. "Old habits. In the basement, if we didn't eat all we were given, we got a beating." He looked at his sandwich. "It's hot, so it's good enough. I went years without a hot meal."

"Years?"

"Guys complained about the food in the Army, but three hots and a cot? Even mediocre food can be good as long as it's hot."

"You ever miss the Army?"

"I wasn't built for it. I'm allergic to people telling me what to do — "

"I can see where that would get in the way."

"It's more common than you might think. In the military, everybody bitches and complains pretty much nonstop. They've all got an idea on how they'd run shit better. The same attitude got in your way, Lily."

I raised a glass in a silent toast. "That's the magic that is me."

Jesus rarely spoke of the traumas he'd suffered in childhood. All I knew was that he'd been locked in a basement and learned English by watching American movies. He hardly ever spoke of his time as a military policeman, either. The details of what he did for the Machine had been off-limits when we were dating, too. We had rarely talked unguardedly. If we had, maybe we would have stayed together. I wondered if we were going to get back together.

Falling in love for the first time is an addictive drug. First love doesn't even feel like a choice. First love happens to you, like a disease. Falling *back* in love, though? That feels dangerous, like an accident you can see coming but are powerless to steer around.

I asked him about the time we'd been apart. He mentioned some trouble in Chicago but glossed over the details. He'd met a guy who gave him a job working security in L.A. He told me stories about the celebrities he saw when he worked as a bodyguard.

He never talked about himself, only funny things others said and did. I could tell there was still a lot he wasn't ready to tell me. That felt okay for the moment. I enjoyed the relaxed moment between us,

Then he ruined the light mood. "Once upon a time, I dreamed you and I would get married and retire to Florida. When I was recovering, I thought about you and me here, in a place like this." He looked around. "Well, maybe not exactly like *this*. The food was better and the place was fancier but it was you and me in Florida."

"You and me in Florida. Were you picturing you and me in the God's waiting room part? Or the meth and oxy part?"

"I was thinking sunshine and easy days, like where the tourists go."

We'd often spoken of getting away from New York before the Machine blew up. I never really thought I'd leave New York then. I told him so, thinking he might cool his jets about getting away together.

"I miss walking around Central Park with you," he said.

"What do you miss about New York that doesn't have to do with me?"

He gave me a blank look.

"Nothing? Really? Don't be sappy."

"I'm not sappy. I'm sentimental."

"You're mental."

"I'm romantic."

"Seriously, name one thing about New York that you miss that doesn't have anything to do with me."

"I miss the early mornings when the City is waking up."

"What? Did you get that from a Woody Allen movie or something?"

"Okay. Truth?"

"Truth."

"I miss getting up early in the morning to go buy weed in Washington Park."

I laughed. Jesus looked relieved. That's when I remembered how happy I was when we were together. We laughed a lot.

Jesus Diaz always seemed so confident and sure of himself, even when things went wrong. That's one of the things that made him stand out in a crowd. A lot of guys in the Machine wanted to date me but most of them were terrified of pissing off my father. Of those that did dare to come sniffing around, only Jesus came at me without hemming and hawing about it.

The first time we spoke was at the same funeral reception where I learned the meanings of different kinds of gunshot wounds. Jesus flat out admitted he was in lust with me. He predicted he would probably fall in love with me, too. "That might take a few seconds of conversation before it gets solid," he said.

That made me laugh. I told him this wasn't the sort of thing he should bring up to a girl at a funeral.

"Yeah, that's enough," he said.

"That's what I'm saying," I said.

"No, I mean, I've heard enough. I'm already in love with you."

"That was too fast."

"I'm a smart guy. But go ahead. Take your time. I'll wait for you to catch up and fall in love with me, too."

"You're cocky."

"It's true love, like with Wesley and Buttercup."

"*The Princess Bride?*"

"What else?"

"I love that movie."

"Everybody loves that movie. So…you love me yet?"

"Not yet. Kind of the opposite, so far. You're blowing it."

"You think so? That's okay. I'll wait. I can settle for your lust for a while. I'm comfortable with that, at least for now."

"Easy, tough guy."

"Tough guy? Nah. I'm a lover, not a fighter. A very giving, considerate, fantastic lover."

"Oh, sure, I can tell you're a very sensitive person," I said.

"Absolutely!"

"That was sarcasm."

"I know."

"I know who you are," I told him. "You're the little Cuban. My dad has mentioned you. He says you talk too much."

"Well, yeah, but I'm not that little. And I talk more around your father because I'm not kissing him."

"You aren't kissing me either, Diaz."

"Not yet, but soon, and for the rest of your life."

"That sounds familiar. Is that…? What is — "

"Shades of *Casablanca*, angel. I'll be your Bogey."

And he was.

Something dark lurked beneath our laughter. It was more than just my sense of impending doom. I hadn't realized how sad Jesus was without me. At that moment, I wished Jesus had come with me. I would have been happier crisscrossing Europe with him by my side.

Dad called Jesus "the little Cuban" but he was always much more than that to me.

"Y ou've changed, Jesus. I'm not sure how."

"Broke my nose a couple times since I saw you last."

"It's not that. You're quieter."

"I listen more."

"Meaning you're not as obnoxious."

"Working as a bodyguard taught me to be more polite."

"Is that all it is?"

He shrugged. "The voices in my head ignore me most of the time so I'm ignoring them."

"You seem less full of yourself."

"I got the shit knocked out of me. I thought I could never miss and that I'd never get shot. Then I got shot. That what you mean?"

"Not sure. It's something…do you know? You should know."

He looked away for the first time since we sat down. "To get through the day, I used to imagine myself as somebody else, like everything was a video game or that I was in a movie."

"You don't do that anymore? You want to be you?"

"I still do it but less often. When you spend your life pretending to be someone else, who are you when you scrape all the lies away?"

"Have you been talking to a shrink?" I asked. "You sound like you've been talking to a shrink."

He shook his head and gave me a tight smile. "Not even in Hollywood. Out there, everybody's got an afternoon appointment once a week for a fifty-minute hour. I learned something in Hollywood, though. Everybody is the star of their own movie. I wanted to be the hero — "

"You were an enforcer for the Spanish mob. What are you now?"

"Still the guy who is looking for a way out from under. When I look back on all that's happened, I can't think of a single thing I did that felt like a real choice. It's as if it's all a movie script."

"What do you want to do exactly?"

"What everybody wants: to be free, to write my own script, to have some control of what happens to me. I've spent a lot of time looking backward. That's all done. After we clean up this mess, I'm only looking forward."

I was about to ask him about the future he saw for us. I think he saw that question coming. "Let's not talk about me anymore. What do you miss most about New York, Lily?"

"People watching."

"You can't watch people anywhere?"

"Without all the paranoia, I mean. I watch people for different reasons now. It was fun to sit in the Village, have a latte and make up stories for people passing by."

"No stories now?"

"I always sit with my back to the wall, never to the door. I'm always vigilant, I can never really relax. I watch people's hands more. I'm always on the lookout for panel vans and black SUVs with dark windows."

"Good call," Jesus said. "Especially a dirty panel van. I always think somebody's up to something when I see a dirty panel van."

That made me smile. "You don't miss the Army but do you miss being a cop for the Army?"

"Sometimes. I had a sergeant I didn't get along with. When my review came up, he told me I had too much sympathy for the heads I was supposed to be busting. 'Too much FIDO,' he told me."

"FIDO?"

"Suppose I were to run across a guy smoking a little reefer on the base. Regs are very strict about that sort of thing but I think it's fine. If somebody needs a little weed to help handle life and the demands of the job, makes sense to me."

"Medicinal doses?"

"Right. If you're signed up, you already have a medical condition. We didn't get to enjoy long afternoons and slow lattes in Greenwich Village."

"Yeah, yeah, thank you for your service. What's FIDO about?"

Jesus looked around as if to make sure no one could overhear us. "Suppose a cop sees some minor infraction that, by the book, might cause him or her to exit his or her vehicle."

"But?"

"But getting out of the car is tedious and not everything is worth the trip."

He leaned closer, as if he was about to share a state secret. "Instead of performing his or her duty, said cop might exercise discretion and choose not to be a prick. That's FIDO. It stands for Fuck It, Drive On. Anything that looks like it's more pain in the balls than it's worth? FIDO."

I chuckled and signaled the waiter for another glass of wine. "FIDO should be a life motto for everybody."

"As long as you and I are driving off into the sunset together, I'm good with that."

Jesus looked so serious and all I wanted to do was keep things light. I avoided staring into his eyes too long. When I did, I recognized that feeling of falling. Jesus had pretty eyes and long lashes. I'm a sucker for long lashes.

"Anything wrong?" he asked.

I knocked back the last liquid from my wine glass. "Time to go."

"Want to grab a motel and make sweet love all night?"

"Subtle."

"Okay, I was planning on the sweet love for the second round. First round: mad and passionate."

"Mr. Cocky's back, I see. Just when I was starting to like you again."

"I'm talking mad passion. The bed frame will be broken. Maybe a lamp — "

"Better than a motel, let's go stay among friends."

"You've got friends in Boca? Who? You got grandparents in a timeshare stashed around here somewhere?"

"An old friend in Manalapan. Safest way to stay off the grid and under the radar is to stay with a friend who has a house behind a long driveway and a gate."

"Who are you talking about?"

"Miguel Ochoa."

"Who?"

"A guy I dated briefly."

"Awesome."

"And by 'awesome,' you mean — "

"Shit."

And with that, we set off for Manalapan to hide out at Miguel Ochoa's mansion.

We were very quiet at first. Talking about Miguel was a tripwire and neither of us wanted to risk detonating that emo-bomb. There's a certain inevitability about sensitive topics, though. Once a wound is inflicted, you can't stop touching it and testing it to see if it's still painful. After we were on the road for a few minutes, Jesus asked, "How did you end up down in Manalapan, anyway?"

"After we parted ways in New York, I came here to let the heat die down. I thought I'd be safe for a while but every day I got more paranoid. I went to Orlando and did the whole Disney thing because I knew I could lose myself there. It felt safe. Eventually, I called my mother."

"With the FBI listening?"

"I got around that."

"How?"

"I told her it was her florist."

He quirked an eyebrow at me. "Your mom has a florist?"

"Dad was high up in the Machine, Jesus. That means a lot of funerals. Mom recognized my voice, of course, so she figured my play pretty quick."

"Which was?"

"I told her the flowers she sent to her dentist couldn't be delivered. The office was closed. There was nobody there because the whole staff were out at Dr. Majoopani's father's funeral. I told her she could pick it up and deliver it herself at her convenience if she wanted. She caught the hint and went to the florist."

"She was probably followed."

"Didn't matter. She had a bouquet waiting for her. That one was from me to her."

"And I bet there was a number for her to call on the back of the card."

I nodded. "She called me that night from a payphone."

"The Vasquez women are devious."

"There's a way out of everything."

"I hope you're right. What does this have to do with Manalapan?"

"That's where Mom told me to go. She knew someone — a friend of the family — who could put me up until we could figure a way for me to get out of the country. Once the heat from the FBI died down — "

"We can't hide out in Manalapan," Jesus said. "We need to disappear into a city. A town is way too small."

"My friend's house is big enough you can go to the bathroom eight times and not take a dump in the same toilet for a week."

"Who needs that many bathrooms?"

"Not my point."

"And this guy — "

"Miguel Ochoa."

"Why do I know that name?"

"Like I said, friend of the family."

Jesus looked at me skeptically.

"Okay, he's not just a friend of the family. He's connected."

"You ran from the Machine to the Family? As in Mom and Pop, the Family? With ties to the cartel? Drug running and, oh, for Christ's sake — "

"For your sake and mine, we need to hole up. Miguel's place is safe. The Family isn't exactly a rival to the Machine. They've got different territories — "

"A connected guy from another mob is safe?"

"Relatively. He likes me so he'll have to like you, package deal."

"Everybody likes you, Lily."

"Don't sulk. You got any friends from your childhood in Miami who will let you sleep on their couch?"

Jesus went quiet. Anyone Jesus Diaz ever knew in Miami was dead. He pulled out his new burner phone, looking antsy.

"Who are you calling?"

"An old emergency number. I hope it still works."

"What are you trying for, exactly?"

"Same as always," he muttered. "Salvation."

2 6

Someone answered Jesus' call right away. "Marissa? It's the Second Coming."

There was a pause as Jesus listened. I strained to hear but I couldn't quite catch anything from the other end of the conversation.

"Is this another handyman?" I ask.

He waved me off and I watched the road. We'd been eating up miles and would arrive in Manalapan soon.

"I need a favor from Gaffney," Jesus said. After a long pause, he said, "Then don't call it a favor. I've got money and I know James can help out."

It sounded like it was not working out. Without saying goodbye, Jesus turned off the phone and shoved it into his pocket.

"What was that about?"

"I can't call a handyman. If I get in touch with a local fixer, Denny will know we're back in Florida. That's why I got Reilly to get you a Canadian passport. By now, the Machine is looking for us north of the border."

"Who is Marissa?"

"I ran into a guy on another job a while back. Somebody tried to hire me to do a job. I didn't like it and passed. In fact, I decided to protect the target."

"It was a hit?"

He bobbed his head. "Of a little kid, if you can believe it."

"Brutal."

"That's how I met James Gaffney. I thought he was trying to take over the contract."

"You didn't take him out?"

"That's where things got weird. I took him out for beer and hot wings."

"What?"

"Funny guy, big into baseball. He wasn't going to kill the kid. He'd taken the job to rescue him. I wish somebody like him was around to rescue me when I was a kid in Miami."

"I don't really get it."

"Gaffney relocates kids. He can be salty but if I'd had a guy like that looking out for me back in the day, I wouldn't have ended up stuck in a basement for years. I would have been Annie and Gaffney should have been my Daddy Warbucks. He says it's a hobby that pays well."

"This guy could help us?"

"I thought he could, yeah. His assistant disagrees. Apparently, we're a little old for his target demographic. Gaffney isn't set up to deal with adults and he's off on another job doing God's work. How about we find a motel and chill out and find another way out?"

Jesus didn't want to share me with anyone. He wanted to be the hero who solved my problems. And he really didn't want us to stay with my old flame. "We don't have to be here long. I can get my hands on the memory stick tomorrow."

Jesus was a stubborn guy but so was I. The argument made me feel like we were already boyfriend and girlfriend again, but without the sex.

We arrived in Manalapan and soon turned into Miguel's driveway. We rolled up to the gate and I leaned out to push the button on the intercom.

A guard with a shotgun slung over his shoulder appeared behind the gate's steel bars. He stared at us through mirrored sunglasses. I ignored him and smiled for the camera on my side of the vehicle. "Tell Miguel it's the only woman who ever."

"Whoever?" Jesus looks confused.

"Who, *pause, ever* ...." I explained.

"Who ever what?"

"Never mind. He'll know."

The gate to Miguel's estate slid aside and the tension in my shoulders eased. When I glanced at Jesus, he did his Admiral Akbar impression: "It's a *trap!*"

I hated Jesus' *Star Wars* references.

The guy in the mirrored sunglasses was Bruder. I didn't know what his real name is. At first, I thought Miguel called him that because he was brooding. Miguel explained that Bruder is German for *brother*.

Bruder's hand went to the Bluetooth device in his right ear. He nodded as if whoever was on the phone could hear his brain rattle. The guard pointed us to the front of the house without a word and stayed at his post at the gate. I remembered him because (a) Bruder was a big brute who liked to wear too-tight t-shirts and, (b) he said nothing but yes or no all the time I stayed with Miguel. I was never sure how much English he understood.

A guy in a loud shirt open to the belly button emerged from the mansion's front door. I knew him, too. On our first meeting, he told me to call him Hands. Hairy chests aren't necessarily bad, but his sharp features reminded me of a weasel.

This guy's real name was Hans. He called himself Hands because he got tired of explaining the nuance of his name to women in bars. They often misheard his name when he tried to yell it over blasting trap music.

I thought Hands was a pretty douchey guy and told Miguel so.

"Yeah, but he's European," Miguel had told me, as if that explained why he should keep him around.

"Hands doesn't even have a German accent," I protested. "He grew up in Sarasota Springs!"

"He's got a European *sensibility*," Miguel said. "Look at his iPod. He's got Kraftwerk and Husker Du on infinite repeat."

"Really? How old is Hands?"

"Too old for trying to pick up chicks in clubs but I find him amusing and he knows how to cook."

As Hands approached our vehicle, I saw that he was strapped with a shoulder holster. The grip of a huge revolver stuck out of it. Hands was so slight, it seemed the sidearm weighed him down.

I've known guys who carried guns all my life. There are a few kinds of people who bother with concealed carry. I liked the sane pros, the ones who look at them as tools. A mob guy who knows his business is like any farmer in the Midwest. If he has to shoot a varmint in the henhouse, he's ready, but it's just a tool. Jesus wouldn't take a selfie with his SIG, just like it would never occur to a reasonable person to take a picture with his washing machine. The pros are the most dangerous and effective with a gun in their hands.

Hands was such a poser, he didn't even conceal his carry. He probably hadn't practiced on a gun range since he first got that big Smith & Wesson. Maybe that hand cannon gave him comfort but, like his open shirt, it was definitely for show.

Hands strutted around Miguel's estate, fetching drinks, smoking salmon and grilling prime rib. That big Smith & Wesson must have gotten in the way of his real duties.

Some gun owners whip out their penis substitute at any opportunity, proud of their toy. They've got more guns than brains and can't wait for an opportunity to use their noisemakers. These guys think they don't have to take shit from anybody because of those stiff rods in their pockets. Never mind all the gastric bypass surgery, sitting still and shopping at Mr. Big & Tall. They're heroes!

When I see guys who think they're cowboys, I want to take them aside and let them know the West has already been won. It's over and they should get over it and invest in a personality.

I had found that Miguel often surrounded himself with people who were either stupid or coarse. I suspected he felt his friends made him look smarter and smoother by comparison.

I felt safer with Jesus around and it wasn't his SIG that made him tough. He was gentle with me and carried himself with quiet confidence, as if he could handle whatever problem arose. His jealousy of Miguel was a little flattering but, ironically, stepping back onto the estate in Manapalan reminded me why I preferred Jesus Diaz.

Seeing these guys strutting around Miguel's estate with their weapons on display reminded me of Carmine Malgor and the first time I shot a man. Mostly, I meant to shoot him.

Carmine Malgor seemed kind enough, at first. I called him Uncle Carmine but he wasn't really my uncle. My mother told me that my father's friend was a useful person to know because he had connections who could get weapons at a reasonable price and sell them at a high markup. I don't recall my father saying much about Uncle Carmine except that he was an earner.

Carmine handed me my first pistol when I turned twelve. Dad allowed it because he was terrified of what would happen when puberty hit me smack in the vagina. Judging by my budding young breasts, the boob fairy was about to make a delivery. My mother has an impressive, heavy rack. The things my Dad loved most about Mom — "Fun bags!" — terrified him about his daughter.

Mom thought gun training with Carmine was a good idea. She didn't want me to think guns were mysterious things. As Mom put it, "A pretty girl's gotta know more than how to knee a pervert in the balls." No daughter of hers was going to shoot herself or anybody else by accident. (Shootings with intent and purpose, she was okay with.) Besides, everybody we knew was strapped. Guns were part of the Machine's gears.

Every Friday afternoon for a year, Uncle Carmine picked me up after school and took me to his firing range for lessons. He instructed me in the proper use and care of every weapon in his private arsenal. I liked Carmine. He smelled of gun oil, was a kind teacher and every lesson ended with us going out for gelato. I thought he was a sweet old guy, but he only knew two topics thoroughly. He could talk about guns endlessly. His other hobbyhorse was how the government was going to try to take all his weapons away someday. Uncle Carmine was sure there would be a civil war was coming. "The moment *that* war is declared and the curtains come down on bullshit society? Hoo, baby! Watch out!"

Carmine couldn't wait for the apocalypse. "The safeties will come off, just you wait! You can see it all, coming up from underneath. The projects are going to explode and it's all going to boil over. The anger is just simmering now, but the heat on that pot is climbing up and up. On the day it finally comes to pass, I'll walk down the middle of Fifth Avenue and shoot any fed or cop or *whatever* that gets in my way."

I didn't figure out for a while that when Carmine said "whatever," that was his code for *black*. He was so polite and friendly, it hadn't occurred to me he wouldn't like that many of my friends at school were black.

"It's going to be huge!" he enthused. "When that day comes, you better be ready, Little Lily. You see all those homeless people out there? *That's* the real zombie apocalypse. When they start coming at Wall Street with lice in their hair and bed bugs in their clothes carrying pitchforks and torches, the government will lose control. All illusions will evaporate and the president's last official act will be to deputize guys like me to clean up the mess."

The guys in the Machine called him Carbine. It was one of those jokes that was really meant to be taken seriously. They thought he was a little too obsessed with the end of the world, too.

Dad seemed to tolerate my gun trainer well enough. However, when Uncle Carmine warmed to his favorite subject for too long,

Dad would begin to sigh. My father always ended those conversations in the same way. "Carbine, get yourself to a Mets game. Please."

"And why should I go to a fuckin' Mets game?"

"'Cause you need a new hobby. Goddamn! Read a book or somethin'!"

Unfortunately for Uncle Carmine, his personal apocalypse came in a way neither of us expected. One day after we'd finished our gelato, he took me back to his place to show off his new Russian machine gun. My boob fairy had arrived by then and her gifts were generous: My C cups runneth over. Uncle Carmine noticed and he wasn't supposed to. My new cleavage transformed Carmine into Uncle Bad Touch. I was unarmed at the time but, no matter, I still had knees.

He went down hard. I ran out of Carmine's house crying. I started walking and thought about calling my mother for a ride home. Then I realized I'd left my purse behind. I didn't know what to do so I went back to Carmine's and rang the bell. He answered the door naked, wincing and rubbing his balls. "You hurt me, Little Lily. That wasn't nice. You come back to kiss it better?"

I ran past him to get my purse. I was shaking and crying. Carmine started laughing. I'd never heard him laugh like that. It was an ugly sound and I wanted it to stop. He grabbed me and spun me around. He tried to force me to my knees. I fell back. The air went out of me and he was on top of me.

"You came back, Little Lily. You come back, you get what you get. No excuses later! You came back!"

My hand closed on the pistol he'd given me. I shot him through the top of his right foot. Years later, Jesus and I watched *Goodfellas* together and I had a flashback when Joe Pesci shoots the waiter in the same spot.

In *Goodfellas*, Spider goes down and he doesn't even scream in pain. Carmine screamed a lot. He also rolled off me. He was too fat to get his hands around the spurting wound easily but he tried.

Carmine was even less polite after that. He called me nasty

names while I looked down at my ruined purse. A lipstick slipped to the floor out of the hole my shot had made.

We didn't have math problems like this in school but I learned a single 9mm round makes a bigger hole in a purse than nine millimeters. That made me mad. When I knelt on his chest and put the muzzle to his forehead, Carmine suddenly stopped cursing me. He went very still.

"You know the rule," he said. "Never draw a weapon unless you're prepared to use it. You ready to kill me for horsing around, Little Lily?"

With the gun pressed to his head, I started to shake. I was sure this was one of those situations where Dad would approve of being proactive. My mother would have killed Carmine three or four times already.

Before I finished shaking, the bastard smiled and told me he knew I couldn't pull the trigger. "Lots of gun training but you've still learned nothing from the master, huh?"

He tried to grab the gun away from me. I squeezed the trigger and the worst thing in the world happened to Uncle Carmine. That round took off his right index finger.

I thought he'd screamed before, but the sound he made next reminded me of agitated goats at the Bronx Zoo. While Carmine was busy freaking out about that, I stomped on his left forearm. I wasn't crying anymore. I was smiling. "Don't call me Little."

I pushed the muzzle to his left index finger and fired my first truly intentional shot, filled with purpose. When I left, I took his trigger fingers with me to make sure he couldn't get them reattached and come after me.

I told my mother as soon as I got back home. I opened my bag and she saw the hole. I'd plugged the hole with tissues. Mom looked in the bloody clump of tissues and found Carmine's index fingers. She took them and walked away for a moment without a word. I heard the toilet flush twice.

A few minutes later, Mom returned and gave me a hug. Then she called my father and handed the phone to me. "Tell him what you told me."

"Everything?"

"Everything," she said. "Your father will not be angry. Not at you."

My father listened. He didn't interrupt me, which was unusual. I repeated everything that had been said and left out nothing. When I was done, Dad told me he loved me and that this would never happen again. "You will never have to worry about Carmine. I'll have a talk with him. Put your mother back on the phone."

Mom took the phone from me and said, "Take care of it or I will." After a long pause, she said, "If you have to get permission from Vincent Lima, then get it. I don't care what the boss says, though. Carmine has to go away, somewhere he'll never come back from. Take care of it! Do you hear me, Pete?"

Then she hung up without waiting for her husband's reply.

"What does that mean? To take care of it?" I asked.

"It means you don't know and you don't want to know. You did right, girl. Any man lays a bad hand on my baby pulls back a quivering stump. You remember that. You did right. Now go have a long hot shower. When you're ready, you and I are going shopping for another purse. And more ammo."

The name Carmine Malgor was never spoken again in my house. Later, I recognized some of his weapons among the Machine's crew. His body was never found.

A voice came to me from far away. Jesus squeezed my hand. "Lily? You okay?"

Hands was smiling and waving at me from the front step.

"Just spaced out a moment." But I was thinking about how I shot a man for the first time when I was thirteen years old. I'd shot a lot of men since. How many more before I returned to freedom and safety? When would my private apocalypse be over? Once an apocalypse starts, does it ever really end?

29

W e found Miguel snoozing by the pool in a lounge chair. The back of the mansion was huge with a wooden fence around the perimeter broken only by iron gates. A water fountain bubbled in a corner to my left. I wondered if the groundskeepers who visited once a week had any idea Miguel was a connected guy who managed the Family's smuggling operations.

Two hotties — one blonde and one redhead, both topless — splashed each other in the piano-shaped pool in the center of the yard. When they spotted Jesus and me, their laughter died and they stared at us, brows furrowed.

"Boss?" Hands nudged Miguel. "Somebody's here to see you. It's a nice surprise. I saw her on the gate camera and I buzzed her in right away. You'll like this."

Miguel roused slowly, lazy from the heat. As he squinted up at me, a big toothy smile spread across his face. "Lily!"

"Hi, Miguel. You're looking well." And he was. He'd lost weight since I saw him last. Shirtless and tanned, his shoulders look like he's been hitting the gym hard.

He looked from me to the women in the pool and beckoned Hands. Hands bent forward and Miguel whispered. The goon straightened and turned to the bimbos. "Hey, pretty ladies! Come with me, please!"

The women looked at each other without moving.

"C'mon, *c'mon!*" Hands snapped his fingers and headed to the back of the house, assuming they would do as they're told. Instead, they ignored him and eyed Miguel. They knew where the money came from.

Miguel clapped his hands and pointed like he was a lifeguard ordering naughty children out of the pool. They both made faces at me and left without a word. On the way out, the women glanced back at Jesus as they retrieved their bikini tops.

Miguel rose to envelop me in a bear hug. He kissed my cheek, pulled back to look me up and down and then hugged me again, tighter the second time. Then he gave Jesus the once over, as if he was an alien who just teleported in from out of nowhere. "Who's your friend?"

"Miguel Ochoa, meet Jesus Diaz. I told you about Jesus. He got me out of New York."

"Got you away from the Machine, huh?"

I frowned at Miguel, hoping this wouldn't turn into a pissing match.

"You're the hit man, right?"

"I prefer the term conflict resolution counselor," Jesus said, "but you can think of me as Lily's boyfriend."

At first, I wondered if I heard right. He did not say *ex*-boyfriend.

Miguel stuck out a hand. "Boyfriend?"

"Yup." Jesus didn't crack a smile.

"Lucky man. Good luck taming her."

"Nobody tames a woman like Lily. You just hold on for the ride and be glad you're the one she chooses to be with. If you got a problem with me, we could settle it with a dance battle or something."

I rolled my eyes at Jesus. He was being funny but his delivery was deadpan and he still hadn't taken Miguel's hand.

Miguel seemed to consider this. "Well, any friend of Lily's…"

Jesus finally did accept Miguel's handshake but both men stood ramrod straight. It was as if they were in a contest to see who had the best posture. The subtext was not subtle. They were acting like I was some sort of prize to be won.

"Boys? *Ahem.* We need to talk."

Miguel held up one index finger as he picked up his phone. "Bring us a tray of mojitos, Hands. And make sure the guest rooms have fresh towels and whatnot. Lily and her friend will be staying." His gaze slid up and down my body slowly. "I hope for a good long visit."

This sort of bullshit is what drove me away from Miguel. He was nice to me, always very attentive and complimentary. That was what clued me in on the problem. He told me ten times a day how beautiful I was, but he never gave me any indication he thought I was smart. I'm not one of those bitches who goes topless in the pool, vying for the title of Trophy Wife #3.

Still, I looked around and I understood the attraction. Even the rich people I knew in New York lived in small houses and tiny apartments. Life is lived on a different scale in Manalapan. Miguel was a man of leisure. Anyone who hooked up with him and won the ring would graduate out of the Wage Ape Club forever.

Regular houses have backyards. Miguel's mansion had *grounds*. A stairway to the beach stood beyond the pool. Miguel's backyard was the Atlantic Ocean. His was a life without limits and he had earned it. He owned airplanes because he had taken risks. He had learned to fly in the Navy. When he got out, he went on smuggling runs back and forth from Honduras until he could buy more planes and get other men to take the risk for him.

By the time I'd first met Miguel, he sat on Manalapan's library board, hosted golf tournaments for charity and bought bulletproof vests for the dogs on the local police force. As far as Manalapan was concerned, Miguel Ochoa was an upright citizen. As far as the local cops were concerned, he was a friend they were willing to leave alone.

Miguel smiled at Jesus and waved toward the beach vaguely. "Yanni lives just up that way," Miguel announced this to everyone who met him for the first time.

"Yanni? Really?" Jesus said the right words, but his tone told Miguel he didn't give a shit. Jesus grew up with nothing. He always wanted money but he also seemed to look on anyone who had already achieved wealth with visible distaste.

Miguel's smile looked genuine when he looked my way so I stepped in and gestured for the guys to sit at the table under the big umbrella. Hands emerged from an opening in the glass wall at the back of the house. He strutted toward us briskly, as if he had to go pee. He carried a tray with three tall mojitos, a bowl of limes and an icy pitcher that sweated in the Florida heat.

As Hands set the tray down, Miguel slapped his hands away and told him to start working on dinner. "You two like lobster? I just had some flown in from Maine today. I was in Paris last week. The lobster there was over a hundred dollars a pound. I should have packed up a bunch of our lobsters, taken them with me and sold them. I could have paid for the trip with lobster!"

"Before you take us in, you should know the whole score," I warned.

Miguel took a sip of his mojito and grabbed another slice of lime to squeeze into his glass. "You mean how the Machine is looking for you and the FBI wants your boyfriend real bad?"

"So you've heard."

"I hear lots of things but, for an old friend like you, Lily, I don't have to do anything about everything I hear."

I guess that was the right answer because Miguel and I heard a click just then. It was Jesus. He'd had his SIG out, under the table. He slid his weapon back into his belt.

Miguel wasn't offended. In fact, he laughed hard.

"It's good to be among friends," Jesus said. His tone when he spoke the word "friends" was the same as when he said, "Yanni? Really?"

"Nice suit," Miguel told Jesus. "You must be sweating like the devil in that."

Jesus lifted his glass in a quick salute to our host. "The devil prefers Armani."

30

A fter a dinner of lobster and naan bread, I went back to my
room. Jesus followed. I left him to have a shower, careful to
lock the door behind me. I didn't hear him try the knob,
but I knew Jesus. I'm sure he tested it out to see if I was leaving an
open invitation. The truth was, I hadn't decided yet. I took a change
of clothes into the bathroom with me. When I came out, I was fully
dressed, instead of wrapped in a towel. I caught a flicker of disap-
pointment in Jesus' eyes. Avoiding the bed, I sat in a chair by the
desk.

Jesus looked uneasy.

"What is it?" I asked.

"You sure you can trust Miguel?"

"He treated me okay last time."

"You were alone and, I'm guessing, frolicking in the pool, last
time."

"Don't bust my balls, Jesus. Tomorrow, you and I will go to
Miami. I'll scoop the memory stick and some cash from my safe
deposit box. We'll enjoy some breathing room and you'll have the
bargaining chip you need to get Denny off our backs. What's your
pitch to Denny?"

"Simple. We've already got the skim. That memory stick is worth a lot more than the dough. I'll tell him the price of the stick is the skim you've already got and our freedom. We mail him the stick and everybody walks away. Nobody dies."

"Nobody dies. There's a new and fresh idea."

"It sounds reasonable, doesn't it?"

"It would be smart for Denny to leave well enough alone. Too many people have died already. The cost-benefit analysis works in our favor, especially if we hold on to a copy of the data on that stick. We give him the carrot — "

"But beat him with the stick. That's an even better idea," Jesus said.

"From what Miguel said, the Machine has already reached out to the Family. People know what I've got on them."

"And since I haven't checked in with Denny since London — "

"By now there's a bounty on your head, too."

"There's always a bounty on my head," Jesus replied. "The FBI should have given me a medal for my services in Chicago. Instead, they hold a grudge."

"The heat must have come down," I said. "Otherwise, they would have caught you by now."

"Everywhere I go, explosions happen. They called it terrorism, even if the things that blow up aren't all my fault."

I gave him a hard look. "Aren't they?"

"Not all ... not *technically*."

"Convincing."

He shrugged and pulled off his tie. Then he began unbuttoning his shirt. He stared into my eyes as he did it. This was new.

"Before we go any further," he said, "I need to explain something. I never told you everything about what happened to me in Miami."

"You called that ancient history."

"It's still with me. I have changed but it'll always be with me. I need to tell you because this is about trust — "

"I can trust you, Jesus. I know that."

"I want you to know I trust you, even more than I did before," he said. "I had some issues I was dealing with. I've gotten better at dealing with them. When we were in New York, you wanted more closeness in our relationship."

"Intimacy, yes," I agreed. "That was always your issue." Jesus could talk movies all day and night but when it came to anything personal, something real about himself, he went mute.

"You complained that I always wanted to make love fully clothed."

"Yeah, or in the dark or with me blindfolded," I said. "We don't have to go over old ground. I'm not kink-shaming you or …."

"This is me, Lily."

He pulled open his white linen shirt and I got my first real inkling of all he'd been hiding for so long. My jaw went slack. Two bullet wounds scarred his side. His torso was covered with scars and each scar was identical. Crucifixes were burned into his skin. He had never shown me the extent of his scars.

"I was ashamed. I was just a kid then — "

"The people who did this to you are dead, yeah?"

Jesus nodded.

"Good. If they weren't already dead, we'd have to go find them. I'm glad you showed me. You never had to hide them, you know."

"I know that now. I had a mental block. I was tortured and holding onto it. The way I dealt with my problems, that was all about me, not you."

I understood. I'd never told Jesus about Uncle Carmine, either. "I'm glad you're past it," I said.

He pulled me up from the chair and I ran my hands over his muscular chest. I closed my eyes and ran my palms gently over his torso, almost tickling. His scars were a kind of Braille and every word spelled pain. I kissed his lips, slow and soft. For the first time in a long time, we didn't have to hurry.

"Jesus?"

"Mm?"

"You were always so shy before."

"I'm still shy. I don't think I'm up to walking down the beach in a banana hammock. With all these crosses, people will think I'm trying to start a cult or something. I'll scare children."

"Children, maybe, but I'm not a child. I'm not scared."

"Are you ever scared of anything, Lily?"

"Sure, I am. I'm scared all the time. The trick is not to show it. Like you, now. You're scared."

"How'd you know?"

"All the time we were together, you never took your shirt off to make love. And now, here you are, ready for action. It's a brave thing, but it was so difficult for you before, it's still gotta be tough. Am I right or am I right?"

"You're right."

"You don't have to be scared of me."

"You're the only one I can be honest with like this."

"Enough talk. Shut up and kiss me. Show me. Aren't you in a rush to get me naked, too?"

He smiled. "You know you never need to ask that. Everything I ever had that was good was taken from me. Every time I'm beaten down, I think of the good times we had together."

"Good," I said. "I think we should start with me doing that thing where I lock my ankles behind your head."

He laughed. I teased his lips with mine as I opened my blouse and pressed my breasts into his chest. I could feel the subtle topography of his old burns. I wanted him to know his scars were all okay by me. "I will kiss every hurt away. I promise. You're a new man since New York, Jesus."

"Have you noticed? I've been with you for days. Haven't killed anybody yet."

I kissed him again and nipped at his lower lip before taking his hard-on in my hand. "It's been a long time since we were together. You will have to be reevaluated on your performance." I took him in both hands. "You seem up to it."

He slipped one hand under my waistband. He touched me gently and with expertise. I began to pant. He remembered how I liked to be touched. His tongue found my nipples and he tugged at them with his lips in the way I needed. His breath came faster and, without a word, we both slowed our movements. We wanted to make this night last. We couldn't slow the Earth's spin but we could take our time.

Slow and deliberate, inch by inch, we worked together to pull the rest of my clothes off. Then he stepped to pick me up and lower me onto the bed.

It was not like old times. It was better. For the first time, Jesus let himself be vulnerable. It frightened me a little, too, how different he was. Jesus Diaz had never allowed himself to be vulnerable before. We were not strangers, but we were somehow new to each other. Was he as good a hitman as he was in New York when I knew him? I didn't know yet but I was certain he was a better man.

Jesus kissed his way down my torso and all my thoughts and fears were obliterated. Deep in my belly, I felt an exquisite ache. My want grew to an urgent need. I urged him on, demanding satisfaction. I needed to come as much as I needed oxygen.

Finally inside me, our pace began to speed up. With a sharp intake of breath, my eyes rolled back and I let out a long, low moan. My moans grew as we worked together, climbing the mountain to orgasm. The first time I climaxed, we were still making love. The second time, he flipped me over and it was a good, hard and frantic fucking like it should be. Making sweet love is fine but to my taste, when it's done right it looks like fucking.

I briefly wondered if Miguel or Hands or Bruder could hear us. It didn't matter, though. Nothing else mattered that night. In the privacy of my room, Jesus and I were no longer killers on the run. We were safe and free and I wanted more. I wanted thousands of nights like that and I wanted to spend them all with Jesus.

High on our lovemaking, I fell back onto the pillow, sweaty and smiling, more confident than ever that everything was going to work out. Big Denny De Molina would take the deal. Then Jesus and I would be on our way to French Polynesia.

But how often does any plan go that smoothly?

31

The next morning at dawn I rode him again so slowly, it was almost mean. I enjoyed teasing him. We got to the peak together and collapsed back into sleep for another hour. Then I remembered I wanted to be at the bank the minute it opened. "C'mon. Let's get this new life started."

He was shaving in the shower when I started to worry about what I had to lose. Doubt has a nasty habit of creeping in that way. "Denny *will* take the deal, right?"

Jesus peered out at me from the steaming shower. "No Plan B. I'm banking on Plan A. My name will be on that stick, too, you know."

"That's a reason Denny should trust that you won't turn it over to the FBI."

"And?"

"We'll have to edit you out, just in case we have to pull the pin on that grenade."

"That's a happy thought," he said. "Safety first."

"Maybe we should have a Plan B," I said.

"What are you thinking? Go the Sammy the Bull route and testify? Go into WITSEC and end up like Henry Hill at the end of

Goodfellas? I don't think either of us is built to become an ordinary schmuck somewhere in Iowa. We can't really rat out the Machine, Lily."

"No rats," I said. "That's the code, I know."

"We'd be better off taking the money and running away and hoping Denny never finds us. Didn't work out so well for Jason Bourne and his girlfriend, though."

"Jason Bourne?"

"*The Bourne Supremacy.* Tell me you didn't miss that one."

"Missed it."

"When all this is over, there are some serious gaps in your cinematic education we have to fill. You can't be a master assassin and not know all things Ludlum."

"I'm looking forward to starting the part of my life where I'm not striving to be a master assassin, actually. Getting out of New York was good for me. I want to see more of the world. I want to believe in a world without the Machine. I want a utopia where everybody's innocent and nobody would dream of slitting my throat. Let me be a tourist forever. I want to forget everything my mother ever taught me. With enough good, I think I'll be able to let go of the bad."

"New York was all bad?"

"The parts with you were good," I admitted. "But I've got a lot of other stuff I want to forget."

Maybe swimming in blue, tropical water would allow me to forget the sickening smack of Lonnie's head when he hit the floor. Hang gliding might be enough to erase the Ginger Assassin's one-eyed dead stare. I wanted the world that civilians think they have. I wanted to be around people who would never threaten me or give me cause to be the one holding the bloody knife or the hot pistol. I wanted to be the kind of woman who is happy instead of angry. I wanted to be Little Lily again, before the guns, before Uncle Carmine's missing fingers. I was pretty fucked up by most standards, but to be fair, most people didn't face my problems.

To erase so much, it was clear to me that to get that new life, I had to walk with Jesus. He was forgiving. He knew where I came from and what I needed.

"I want to walk along the edge of an active volcano," I said. "I think tourism might be the cure for my PTSD."

Jesus nodded. He understood. I loved him for that.

I t was just past noon when I walked into my bank in downtown
Miami. The street was crowded, but the heat made everyone
slow. In New York, everyone is in more of a rush. Here, if
someone walked fast, it was because they were exercising in that
vague, ineffective way of people with good intentions who aren't
really serious.

I left Jesus with the car in a parking lot across the street. I
would take care of business at the bank while he was on
overwatch.

The bank's air conditioner was working so hard, it felt like it
could snow. That was welcome when I passed through the front
door but by the time I got in line I was too cold. The cranked air
conditioning wasn't for the benefit of customers, anyway. The
bank's staff were dressed as if we were hundreds of miles north,
each one locked inside an uncomfortable suit or a knock-off dress.
They all had that earnest look of strained concentration that
suggested they were working hard at math problems, possibly
constipated.

At the front desk, I met a middle-aged woman who wore her
hair so short she looked like she just got out of boot camp. The

severe cut emphasized the fact that she had a lot of face and all of it was sour, as if she'd licked a lemon lollipop from the gutter.

I'd rented one of the bigger safe deposit boxes and left enough in my account to cover its cost for five years. After a mercifully brief exchange in which I flashed a fake ID and my safe deposit box key, I followed her into the vault. I'd made sure to get a box that was high off the ground. Safe deposit robberies are rare. Flooding is more common. It seemed a silly concern at the time but I hadn't known if or when I would return. Miami is in the climate change flood zone. Panama Bob's memory stick was my last ditch safety net and I wanted to make damn sure it was where I left it, dry and secure.

You're not supposed to store anything in a safety deposit box that is organic or anything that could explode. I'd taken precautions. I'd chosen a small branch of a small chain of banks. It was unlikely anyone would perform such an expensive test, but if anyone had scanned for gunpowder residue, my package would not set off any alarms. The trick was nothing special: two pieces of Tupperware, one inside the other and lined with tinfoil. I'd washed the outer container thoroughly and handled it with disposable gloves.

The woman with the sour face turned her key and I turned mine. She tried to flash me a smile but those muscles were so atrophied, her attempt came off as a weak lip spasm. She left me alone with the contents of the box behind a little blue curtain.

There were only two items in the box. I'd put the memory stick in a small plastic bag (a double precaution against flooding). The other object was a gift from my mother on the night of my eighteenth birthday. We'd had the whole family over. There'd been dancing, though the music was mostly chosen by my parents and my dance partners were cousins and distant relatives. Still, it had been a good night. My relationship with my parents was peaceful then. Things must have been going well at my father's work, too. He wasn't drinking much and Mom wasn't irritable. I remember my mother and father danced a lot that night. That made their choice of music okay with me. I liked them both more when they didn't bicker.

That night as I got ready for bed, a soft knock came at my door.

It was my mother with a white box wrapped in red ribbon. She laid it on my bed without a word.

"I thought I'd gotten all my presents."

"This one is a secret, from me to you."

"You gave me lots already." And she had. After I'd blown out my candles, the chocolate fudge cake had been served. My parents had handed me two envelopes. One contained a wad of cash. The other was a university brochure. I'd planned to go to Columbia and they were going to pay my way.

"Open it," she said.

I did as I was told. It looked like another cake box. It wasn't a cake. It was a little automatic.

"It's a Walther P38K with a short barrel, only three inches," Mom said. "The grips are custom hardwood, 9mm parabellum. No serial number, see?"

"Um…thanks, Mom." I wondered how many other girls my age in New York got a pistol for their eighteenth birthday. Pistols might be pretty common in Texas but not in the Bronx. I imagined a lot of girls in my upscale neighborhood got a copy of Dr. Seuss' *Oh, The Places You Will Go!*

"It's a nice little gun," she told me. "I wanted you to have it because it belonged to my mother."

"*Abuela* had a pistol? Why? She was the wife of a florist."

"Your *abuela* ran numbers in Queens. That's how they could afford that shop."

"You never told me that."

"She went to jail, too."

"For gambling?"

"For keeping her mouth shut about the gambling." She picked the gun out of the box and handed it to me.

Though the Walther was small, its heft surprised me.

"I'd hate for you to lose it but if you have to use it, if something happens, you know you'll have to ditch it in the river, right?"

"What's going to happen?"

"Nothing's going to happen … probably. I'm not saying when, I'm just saying, *if*. You travel back and forth from university…maybe you get your own place…who knows? A young girl in the city, you never know what anybody's going to do. Maybe you have to use it. If you do, you wipe it and lose it, understand. Your *abuela* filed the numbers off this gun herself."

A few things made more sense now. My father never said how he got into the Machine. I had a good guess now. Dad had a good head for numbers. When he became a bookie, he wasn't a rebel or a criminal, exactly. He was just joining the family business.

"You're one of us. You stick around us, you're protected. Nobody can touch you. You go off to school, though— " She tilted her head back and forth and shrugged.

"Mom! I'm not going away to a war zone."

"Everywhere's a war zone," she said. "And not everybody knows who our princess is everywhere you go." She kissed my forehead. "No matter how far from us your life takes us, remember who you are."

Standing alone in a bank vault now, I felt the weight of the Walther in my palm again. I thought hard about who I was and what I'd become. I was the daughter and granddaughter of gamblers. My family counted a crime syndicate as its family, too. New York's Spanish mob is in our blood. We are the Machine and the Machine is us.

At least it was. Since Jesus killed the top soldiers in the Machine and Denny took over, I wasn't family anymore. I was going against the family and willing to become a rat to protect myself.

I tucked the ammunition for the pistol in my purse and took a deep breath. Now that I was armed again, I felt a little better. The weight of the Walther in my hand was a comfort. The weight of the Machine on my shoulders and the price on my head was my curse.

The little memory stick was not so reassuring. If my mother knew I planned to threaten to turn the Spanish mafia over to the feds, she might shoot me. Just a flesh wound, probably. I never said they were monsters. Despite it all, I was still her daughter.

The data on the Machine was my bargaining chip so I guessed that, somehow, I'd become a gambler, too. I had no illusions: The odds stood against me.

33

When I came out of the bank, I had the Walther in my purse and the memory stick tucked into my panties. I had that feeling again, as if I was being watched. I told myself it was probably paranoia. Or maybe it was Jesus' gaze, undressing me with his eyes from across a parking lot. That put a little strut in my stride. Then I spotted two guys in a black car at the entrance to the parking lot.

I tried to take them in at a glance, as if I wasn't worried, staying casual and taking in the sunny day. I looked twice, pausing for a moment as if I was a little lost and searching in my purse for my phone.

The car had Florida plates and it wasn't a rental. The men were young but they had hard faces. Both had thin hair, slicked back. My hands trembled slightly, but I got going, trying to find my strut again. Breaking stride might have tipped them off.

As I approached their car, I noticed they were not talking to each other. They looked wrong to me. It was way too hot for two guys to sit in a parked car with the windows rolled up and the engine off. No engine meant no AC. They weren't talking or looking at each other. Something was up.

The driver looked my way just as I passed, as if he, too, was sneaking a peek and trying to take in everything at a glance. I'd known a lot of young men with hard faces like theirs. Most of those I'd met had worked for my father. One look told me these weren't the kind of guys who know enough to hold back when their testosterone is running high. These were the sort of men who talk when they should listen and their default was to lose control and do something stupid they'd seen in movies.

It occurred to me that Denny De Molina was so desperate to get hold of what was hidden in my panties, maybe he'd put a Disney on me.

When Big Denny brought Jesus inside the Machine, they didn't call him Jesus Diaz. They all called him "the little Cuban." He didn't get a lot of respect, at first. Jesus would say he didn't get any respect at last, either. His first official job for the Machine was to be a Disney. That's not just a Florida term (though some call it being an Eiffel, as in Eiffel Tower).

Jesus had complained to me at the time, "There's this hump in Brooklyn who owes your dad money. Your father's convinced he's going to show at his mother's house. When I asked when, your dad said, 'Someday.' Man, I hate being a Disney."

Naturally, my next question was, "The fuck is a Disney?"

The theory is, if you go to Disney World and stand at the gate and watch long enough, you'll see everyone you've ever known. Everybody goes to Disney eventually. It's a stakeout that feels like it will never end. If the reward is large enough, it makes sense. Sons and daughters always return home, especially for special occasions like Mother's Day, Father's Day, weddings and funerals. Somehow, I was sure Denny knew I'd come back to this bank.

If these men were who I thought they were, they'd want to make sure they would take me in a much more secluded place than a public parking lot. We were next to a busy street. When I looked around, I saw two young women pushing strollers. If the bad guys came at me hard, civilians were in the line of fire. Though the bad guys might not care, they didn't want that kind of attention and the ensuing complications, either.

Were I these guys, I'd want to find where Jesus and I were staying. Or maybe they'd force us off the road on the way back to Manalapan. Then things would get really ugly.

Jesus got out of the minivan and pulled his sunglasses down his nose a fraction. By his eyes, I knew his mood had changed. I recognized that serious look and my pulse jumped to a higher pace. Jesus had been watching and he worried about the men in the car, too. Before I could say anything, he told me, "Got 'em. Two soldiers in the black car by the entrance. They rolled up fast as you were crossing the street going into the bank. They've just been sitting there since. You strapped?"

I nodded. "Something's wrong. I don't like this."

"Me, neither. Borrow your clapper a minute?"

I passed the Walther to him. He left the driver's side door open and pointed me toward the minivan. "Do me a favor? Block their passenger side door. Park it tight."

"What are you going to do?"

"Have a friendly chat."

"What if they're feds?"

Jesus shrugged. "If they're from the mob, they're men with guns hunting us. If they're feds, they're men with guns hunting us. The difference is just politics."

34

I got behind the wheel as Jesus disappeared behind some cars to my left. From where the men sat looking in their rearview mirror, it must have looked like he got into the minivan.

As I pulled the vehicle out slowly, the dude on the passenger side looked back at me. I glimpsed Jesus between cars, keeping low and coming up on the driver's side. When he was almost on top of them, I accelerated. The minivan's tires squealed a little as I skidded to a stop an inch from the passenger side of the black car. I slid over quick so I wouldn't get shot in the head. I needn't have worried. Jesus was already at the window holding my *abuela's* Walther to the side of the driver's neck.

I was too curious to stay put. I got out through the sliding door on the passenger side and came around the back of the black car to lean on the fender. I kept a wary eye for trouble on the street as Jesus relieved the driver of his keys. Jesus waved me forward and handed a couple of .38s back to me.

Until that moment, not a word had passed between Jesus and his captives. These had to be mob guys. Feds would have been pleading and threatening.

Jesus opened with, "How's Denny doing?"

The driver said nothing. He seemed to be concentrating on sweating hard. The passenger was a tough-looking character with thick jowls and a bent nose. I wondered how long he'd been sitting on this bank, enduring the heat, waiting for me and eating cheeseburgers. I'd probably harmed his health already, let alone what Jesus might do to him at any second.

"Denny's concerned," the passenger said. "You seem to be off task, Jesus."

"You know who I am?"

"Everybody in the Machine knows you. You're the guy who chooses pussy over loyalty."

Jesus tossed a nod my way. "You've seen her. You would, too."

The passenger lets out a nervous chuckle at that, but his eyes were on Jesus the whole time. I was pretty sure he not only knew Jesus by sight, he knew his rep.

"Enough of the boy's club shit-talk." I popped open the back door and slid in behind them to point their own pistols at their heads. I didn't know if they knew my rep, but if they tried anything, word would spread.

"I need to talk to Denny," Jesus said. "He needs to come to an accommodation."

The sweaty driver looked up for the first time. "A what?"

"Never mind. We're leaving. I'll reach out to him. You guys stay here and think happy thoughts."

The passenger squirmed in his seat as I pressed the muzzle of a .38 to the back of his head. "Happier thoughts than that."

He stayed still. I could understand why people would like this job. The work appealed to my feminist sensibilities.

"You can't just flake on Big Denny," the passenger said.

"We'll be in touch after I take a few more precautions to make sure things will go smoothly. When you talk to him, tell Denny he doesn't have anything to worry about. C'mon, Lily. Let's go."

"They were going to kill us and now we're just walking away?"

Jesus bounced their car keys in the palm of his free hand. "If we're going to walk away later, we gotta walk away now."

I hesitated. Jesus gave me a warning look. "Lily, play nice. They're only doing their jobs. They're shitty at it but it is what it is. Maybe we can't manage to be polite but let's keep it civil."

"Really?"

"It's not necessary."

I was annoyed at how grateful those humps were when they looked at Jesus. However, I got out and crossed my arms to hide their guns. It's a trick Jesus once taught me. Bodyguards on alert often stand with their arms crossed: The gun hand stays inside the jacket, ready to pull from their shoulder holster. I didn't have a jacket so the pistols went into my armpits.

Jesus bent from the waist, slid his sunglasses down again and winked at our would-be assassins. "I give you your lives as a gesture of good faith. Once upon a time, I was a Disney, too."

The driver looked like he was about to pass out. He nodded a lot. He was delighted that his ordeal would end in a way that wouldn't plaster the inside of his car with brains and gore.

"Take it easy, guys," Jesus said. "Go sit in the shade and have an iced tea before you call Denny. He'll yell at you and call you mean names, but he wasn't here with a gun stuck in his neck, was he? Don't sweat it. People get yelled at and told they're idiots every day. Shouldn't hurt much, unless you think he's right."

He tapped the car roof twice and they jumped. Jesus walked away.

As we got back in the minivan, I turned to Jesus. "I have to ask, when you were recovering from your gunshot wounds in Mexico, did they have the TV on the whole time?"

"Pretty much. Why?"

"That's the second time in the last few days you've given kind advice to men sitting in cars."

"Your point?"

"I think you watched too much Dr. Phil."

"Well, I was wounded, Lily. I couldn't get up to change the channel."

"Yeah, those wounds must have been bad."

He nodded. "Getting shot hurts even more than you think it

does. We're not out of this yet. It could get bloody again and quick. No need to start up trouble on the street in the middle of Miami. We just fled a massacre in one country. Let's not go crazy unless we have to. There are only so many countries to run to."

Our encounter with Denny's humps had me sweating more than the Florida sun. Back in the minivan, I cranked the air conditioning high. I couldn't wait to have a swim in Miguel's pool to cool off. I thought we were headed straight to Manalapan, but Jesus had other plans. Our next stop was the Lincoln Road Mall in Miami Beach. When I asked him what's up, he told me he wanted a smoothie. After I punched him in the shoulder, he told me what he was really up to.

"We're going to the Apple store to buy a laptop," he said. "We need to upload the data to the cloud. Running around with all that incriminating information is too old school. What if someone just takes it away from us? We'd be dead and the Machine's biggest problem is solved. Once we upload it and it's more easily shared, we're safer."

"Yeah, I don't want to rat but we're safer if we put that option on a hair trigger," I agreed. "We could put it into Dropbox and set the files to be shared at a certain date? It's our insurance policy. If we're both alive, the Machine is never exposed."

He glanced at me and smiled. "That's an even better idea. Hey! This is like Tom Cruise's solution in *The Firm*!"

"Oh, for Christ's sake — "

"Just like in the movie!"

"What is it with you and movies?"

He considered this seriously and, after a moment, answered what I meant as a rhetorical question. "You went to school. How much do you remember of high school? Like, what you actually learned and retained, I mean."

I shrugged. "Dunno. I can do math. I liked *To Kill a Mockingbird.*"

"Yeah? How much do you really remember from the book?"

"I know what chifferobe means."

"Yeah? Well, I saw the movie and I remember every moment. You want to hear a few lines? I do a killer Gregory Peck impression."

"No."

"Well, Scout — "

"No!"

He cleared his throat and reddened. After a few miles, he added, "My point is, I had a rotten childhood but I learned English from the movies. Movies were my school and my only escape. I wanted things to make sense the way they do in movies. Real life is so much more…I don't know."

"Convoluted?"

"Yeah." He looked somber.

I tried to lighten his mood. "Bad guys. Gunplay. Looks to me like your life is a movie, Jesus. Mine, too. Careful what you wish for, right?"

"I'm concerned," he said. "Which movie are we in? How does it end? Am I Thelma? Are you Louise? I was hoping for a more *Mission Impossible* vibe."

"Don't drive off a cliff and we'll be fine. I think, so far, this feels like *True Romance.* They end up living on the beach in Mexico, right?"

"Great. Christian Slater gets shot through the eye in that one."

"He gets the girl."

"After getting shot in the eye."

"Cheer up!" I pulled down my dress and flashed Jesus my boobs. He laughed and I laughed, too.

"Lily, if I get shot in the eye in our caper movie, you have to promise you'll flash me every day. And for twice as long since I'll only be able to stare with one eye."

"Deal."

As we pulled into the parking lot at Lincoln Mall, Jesus turned to me. "If we're dead, the information goes out. If I'm dead and Denny kills you, too? Fuck him. I don't care if the feds get every bit of intel on that stick."

Jesus was about to turn off the engine when a red Ford Mustang roared up in front of us. A man I recognize jumped out. It was Webster Ortega, one of my father's men in New York. He'd be working for Denny. I knew because he had a pistol in his fist and it was pointed at my face. Right in my left eye, in fact.

Ortega motioned for me to roll down my window, stepped close to the door and held the pistol in front of his crotch so civilians were less likely to spot the weapon. "Hello again, Lily."

"Hey, Web," I said.

"Hi, Webster," Jesus said. "Long time, no care."

Ortega glowered at Jesus. "Denny says you owe him a phone call."

"Been meaning to get to that. Did I miss his birthday?"

"Den said you forgot all about him, soon as you laid eyes on Lily, I bet. He said you're leaving a mess wherever you go. You were supposed to handle Lily quietly."

"Well, I can be a moaner and a screamer," I said.

"Don't talk like that," Ortega said. "I've known you since you were a kid. It's creepy when you talk like that."

"Not a little kid anymore, Web. Since I don't let anybody walk all over me, I'll talk how I want."

"Let's not make any more messes here," Jesus suggested. "This is a very public place, Web."

"Both hands on the wheel, Little Cuban — "

"Just saying, man, smile, you're on video." Jesus makes a twirling motion with his index finger. "Surveillance cameras, 180 degrees."

It's too hot for a jacket so he stuffed his snub-nosed pistol into his pants pocket. I was nervous but the effect is also comical. It looked like he'd pitched a tent with a fairly disappointing boner.

"Web?"

"Yes, Lily?"

"Remember when I was little and we'd play hide and seek?"

"I was ... what? Seventeen? I remember, sure."

"Remember how when you'd find me, you tickled me and I pleaded with you to stop and you kept going until I got the heebie-jeebies?"

"Yeah, so?"

"I remember, too." I opened my door fast and slammed him in the face.

He was stunned for a second, but either the minivan's door wasn't heavy enough to do much damage or I wasn't fast enough or he was too close for me to get a lot of momentum.

That was the bad news. The good news was he still had his finger on the trigger. The gun went off in his pocket. Webster yelped and bent over, screwing his face into a twist of pain.

People at the entrance to the mall stopped to look our way. I was halfway out of my seat and pulling a .38 as Webster straightened. He punched me in the temple with a brutal left hook, forcing me back into the minivan.

I was stunned for a few seconds. I managed to yank the door shut but dropped the .38 to the floor. Webster got his arm through my open window. I was still scrambling for my pistol when I felt the cold kiss of Web's muzzle against my forehead. I looked up and Jesus had my *abuela's* Walther out, pointed at Web's face.

"Stalemate," Web said.

"Very John Woo cool, yeah" Jesus replied.

"Guys?" I said. "I'd just like to point out that Jesus is right. We're still surrounded by video cameras and a shot has already been fired. Mall security is probably already on the way. This is Florida. They'll be armed to the teeth and itching to shoot somebody."

"Fine. I'll let you live," Webster said. "Just gimme the money or I'll blow your head off right here and now."

"We don't have the money. We have something more valuable. Panama Bob was going to rat out the Machine."

Ortega looked skeptical. "Bob? He went off a high building years ago."

"I know," Jesus said. "Tossed him off myself."

"Whatever he had would be out of date."

"You think so? I have the memory stick and you're on it," I said.

"Show me."

"Lily," Jesus said. "Give the nice man the stick."

He didn't have to tell me twice. I reach into my panties, pulled out the stick and handed it to Ortega.

A crowd had gathered by the entrance to the mall. Several people had their phones out and a couple of old ladies were pointing our way, gesturing dramatically.

Webster looked to them and back to me with a smarmy smile and said, "Run as far as you'd like. The Machine will find you. Rats run but they don't get away."

He stepped back slowly, his gun still trained on me. "Denny's going to love this. Catch you later."

With that, he turned and trotted to the door of the Mustang.

Jesus threw the minivan into gear and floored it, ramming into Ortega. He saw us coming just in time to stumble back. He screamed as we pinned him between our front fender and the Mustang. His gun and the memory stick popped out of his outstretched hands and clattered to the ground.

I jumped out to retrieve the memory stick. He couldn't see me. His eyes were bleeding. It was as if we'd squeezed the bottom of the toothpaste tube too hard.

I remembered this guy laughing with my father on our back patio. He gave Dad an electric carving knife at Thanksgiving and did the honors, using that knife to cut the turkey. Dad called this man a close friend.

When Jesus pulled back, crumpled metal gave a short shriek.

The people watching from the mall entrance screamed, too. I'd say Webster screamed louder than all of them together.

Passersby were already coming our way, too curious to be cautious. Most of them held their cell phones high, cameras recording every moment. Our tires squealed as we reached the exit.

"Rookie mistake," Jesus said grimly. "You do a traffic stop, first thing you do before anything else is get the driver to shut off the engine."

"Webster was never a cop." My hands trembled. It was not cold but I shivered. It was shock. I much prefer pointing the guns instead of having them aimed at me. I prefer shooting the guns instead of running somebody over.

Jesus glanced at me, concerned. "How's your head?"

"Excellent."

"Really?"

"No. My temple's throbbing."

"We'll get some ice for it."

"Stop for that smoothie you wanted and buy me an ice cream sundae. I'll wear it like a hat."

"You could rock that."

"Thanks. What now?"

"Now? Webster will be fine…eventually. Might have to poop in a bag for the rest of his somewhat shortened life, but — "

"No, I mean, what now for *us*, Louise? Want to drive to the Grand Canyon before Harvey Keitel closes in?"

"We'll head back to Miguel's, Thelma. We lay low. We need friendly faces around us until the heat dies down."

"When does the heat die down?"

Jesus shook his head. "Dunno."

I took that to mean never.

We were halfway back to Manalapan before Jesus spoke again. "By the way, on second thought, I'm the Thelma. You be Louise. I am a young and impetuous Geena Davis."

"You're weird."

"You groove on my weirdness. That and salsa dancing is why you love me."

"Yeah." And I did love him. That's the first time since we got back together that I admitted it. It hadn't taken long to feel that again. Second love is like riding a bike, I guess.

"There's something very different about you," I told him.

"Did I get taller?"

"You still haven't killed anybody."

"What? Not satisfied with terrible maiming?"

"No, seriously. You've let three opportunities just whiz by. You haven't killed anyone for me all day. "

"The day's young."

When we pulled in front of the mansion, Miguel stood waiting at the top of the front steps in a Speedo, ready to meet us. "How was your trip, Lily? Fruitful?"

"We got what we needed but more than we bargained for," I said. "Denny had the bank staked out and we were followed."

Hands scurried out and circled the minivan, appearing to inspect the damage. "You aren't going to get your deposit back." Then he got on his hands and knees and reached under the back bumper. When he stood up, he held a small black box. "But not for the reasons you think."

Before I could touch my pistol, Bruder came from behind the vehicle pushing Jesus in front of him. The big man held his shotgun to Jesus' head and he looked pretty pissed about it. He looked at me and said, "Today's the day, Lily."

Miguel pulled a pistol, apparently out of the crack of his ass. He pointed it at me. "We know about the information on the Machine. Bob's widow told us everything. I'll need that information."

"Why?" I asked.

"Why do you think?"

"Denny got to you, didn't he?"

Miguel laughed. "No, sweetie. I got to Big Denny. I also got hold of one of Mom and Dad's boys."

"You called the Family? I don't get it."

"We're going to have an old-fashioned auction. The Family would like to expand its activities in the Northeast. If they have the information about all the Machine's business activities — "

"Then they'll have Big Denny and his crew by the short and curlies," Jesus said. "Panama Bob was a rat. You're a snake, Miguel."

"I'm a capitalist."

"Denny wants me dead," I said. "I thought you cared about me."

"I did." Miguel came down the stairs, his eyes on mine. My eyes were on his pistol. "I probably wouldn't have sold you out if you'd come alone. I protected you once, Lily. When you came to me from New York, I was ready to do your mother a favor. I fell in love with you a little then. When you left, I was heartbroken."

I shrugged. "I didn't want to marry you so now you're okay with me winding up dead?"

"He asked you to marry him?" Jesus was wide-eyed.

"Not now, Jesus!" I exclaimed.

"I was going to let you go, you know," Miguel said. "I was going to help you but I came to your door last night. I heard you in your room with the little Cuban. The very first night you stay in my home and you don't even consider my feelings? You are ungrateful. That was very disrespectful. "

"Fuck you, Miguel."

"Good comeback, Lily."

"I'll save the witty repartee for when I'm kicking your ass."

Miguel scowled and walked up to me. For the second time in one day, a man hit me. He backhanded me across the face and I was knocked to the concrete.

When I opened my eyes, I was at Miguel's feet looking at his neon green Crocs. Miguel's scowl spread into a big smile that mocked me. "Stupid, Miss Vasquez. Really stupid."

The bastard might not be altogether wrong, I thought.

Before Miguel thought to go digging for it, I handed over the memory stick that could put everybody in the Machine away for life.

When I'd left New York, I walked away from my family, the Machine and everything I knew to go find a new life in Europe. I left Jesus Diaz to go his own way despite all he'd sacrificed for me. After that, I'd slept with a man who wore a Speedo and the ugliest shoes on Earth. And he was about to sell me out.

Stuff like this really makes you reevaluate your life choices. Especially when Miguel added, "Big Denny De Molina is coming to the auction personally. He's almost here."

B ruder waved his shotgun around and Jesus and I kept things civil by cooperating. We sat in lawn chairs by the pool and waited for the auction participants to arrive. The auction was scheduled to begin immediately.

Hands brought us mojitos in tall glasses and, if not for Bruder glowering at us, it looked like we were about to host a late afternoon pool party.

Hands gave me a cold facecloth for my swollen lip where Miguel hit me. The creep left a bottle of Advil on the silver tray beside me. "Thanks, but will I still be alive by the time that pill starts to work?"

Hands shrugged. "Take it or not, Lil. Doesn't matter to me."

"That's cold. Since when are you such a tough guy, Hands?"

Miguel raised his hand as if he was the smartest boy in class. "The answer to your question depends on who wins the auction and what they decide to do with you. Don't blame Hands. You're not our concern anymore."

The emissary from the Family arrived first. His name was Mel Fordman, but he introduced himself as International Mel. He wore a white linen three-piece suit. I assumed he was a mob lawyer. He was sweating so heavily, his thin hair was wet and matted down. He mopped his dripping face with his bare hand. I guess the suit was bulletproof — or, more accurately, as Jesus would say — "bullet-resistant."

"They call me Mel," he said, "My mother saddled me with that name. They call me International because I move so many things across the border for the Family."

"It's more accurate to say *I* move the things across borders," Miguel objected. "You just place the orders. *My* guys fly the planes."

Mel ignored Miguel and Jesus and spent too long staring at me. "So, you're Pete Vasquez's daughter. Pleased to make your acquaintance, Miss Vasquez. Friend of mine had some dealings with his boss Vincent Lima long ago. My friend paid back a debt too slow. Vincent sent Pete out to collect. Your father broke one of my buddy's pinky fingers. Chipped a tooth, too."

"Lily's dad didn't like welshers," Jesus said.

International Mel ignored Jesus and kept staring at me. "That same friend with the chipped tooth and the broken pinkies would remember your father well. That friend of mine occasionally supplies ladies for a sheik in Dubai. It would tickle him if I sent Pete Vasquez's daughter his way. Top dollar, too. I wonder if he'd like you, Lily. Can you play nice?"

Before I could tell International Mel that I bite, Jesus broke in, "Oh, no, man. That was what you call a tactical error."

"What?" International Mel looked baffled, as if Jesus had only just materialized out of nowhere.

"You shouldn't have gone there," Jesus said. "Now we're going to have to kill you in a worse way."

"I've heard about you, too, Mr. Diaz. The little Cuban, they called you," the Family's man sneered. "I could get some heavy slack from the FBI if I turned you in. You're a celebrity with those folks. How many federal agents have you killed?"

"That's greatly exaggerated, actually. I got blamed for some stuff that wasn't my fault. I've killed more guys like you than not."

"I'm sure that's an interesting story." International Mel went back to ignoring Jesus and staring at me. The way he looked at me made me want to have one of those industrial chemical showers. I needed serious cleansing, the kind you can only get if you work in a nuclear plant and are exposed to hazardous waste.

"I don't think you like me, Miss Vasquez," International Mel said. "That's kind of rude, considering we just met. Makes me want to own you myself, teach you some manners your daddy never taught."

I began to shake. I knew this feeling. All my boiling murderous rage had burned off the fear. I thought of how I handled Carmine. I was just a kid then. When my chance came, I could deal with International Mel, Miguel and his bodyguards. When my turn came, I'd make my mother proud.

Jesus cleared his throat. "Lily?" he said conversationally. "Remember what your dad used to say about tilt? Try to keep that in mind now."

"Tilt?" International Mel perked up. "What's tilt?"

"It's a gambling term," I explained. "When my father talked about the suckers, he talked about how they went into a downward spiral, betting badly."

International Mel pulled up a lounge chair and sat opposite me. "Explicate."

Bruder frowned and stepped closer, just in case I lunged. Bruder's instincts weren't wrong.

"Yes, tell us all about tilt, Lily," Miguel said. "I like to watch your lips as you talk."

"Let's say we're playing poker. That's all about reading people and managing risk. Now let's say a gambler makes a bet that should go their way but it doesn't. The gambler's confidence goes south. Sometimes that makes them bet even more aggressively to try to make up for their losses. That's tilt. They make more bets and worse bets and screw themselves into a deeper hole. Then they have to walk home from Vegas. To win, you gotta stay cold."

"Cold?" International Mel looked up at the goons and laughed at me. "Poker players want hot hands and hot streaks. Maybe your dad was a better bookie than a card player, huh?"

International Mel was playing to the crowd. I knew what Jesus was up to, though. He was telling me to wait and watch for an opportunity. What that opportunity would be, I had no idea.

"If the hand is hot, that's fine, but your heart has to stay cold," I said. "When you lose your focus and let the last hand you're dealt fuck up the next hand, you aren't playing smart."

International Mel finally looked over at Jesus. "What do you think? I heard you were a hothead, little Cuban."

"I'm cool." Jesus looked off to the back gate, seeming to ignore International Mel.

"Look at me when I'm talking to you, boy."

Jesus didn't flinch. "I don't like being called that. Boy. Somebody else called me that. It didn't end well for them."

"Uh-huh. *Geez,* Jesus! Should we tie you up? You still talk like a man who thinks he's dangerous even though this big sumbitch is standing right there with a shotgun."

Jesus didn't even glance at Bruder. "Soon, my brother, Big Denny De Molina is going to walk through that gate. Miguel made a mistake calling you and you made a mistake coming. The Family wants leverage over the Machine. I know Denny. I've known him since he was a kid. Big Denny is not going to let your dreams of domination come true. You think he's going to take getting black-mailed by a guy like you? You think he's going to accept an auction to get what's his? The Family must not give a shit about you to send you here, to play into Miguel's little moneymaking scheme — "

"It'll be fine." Miguel rubbed his hands together. "It's business and we're all businessmen."

"It's not going to go down like that," Jesus said. "I've known him when he was Little Denny De Molina. He's not going to take any encroachment on his territory from the Family. And he's not going to like you for setting up the auction, Miguel. Not one bit."

"Stupid. Denny will pay big for you and Lily and the data. Even if your guy doesn't win the auction, feel free to drive up the price."

"Then the Family will want you dead, Miguel."

Bruder and Hands looked at their boss. They both looked uneasy.

"It's fine," Miguel insisted. "The Family needs my planes — "

"Yeah? None of your pilots could take your spot in the chain of command for half the price?" Jesus asked. "You did not think this through."

Despite his tan, I saw doubt creep into Miguel's face. "You okay?" I asked. "You're looking a little pale."

Jesus finally turned to Miguel and smiled. "You didn't know Denny. When you're with Denny and you think all's well, you're already fucked. You just don't know it, yet."

"Funny," Miguel said. "That's what Denny said about you."

Jesus smiled wider. "You should have turned us over to Denny as soon as we showed up. Denny would owe you and you might have even bargained for a piece of the Machine's international transport business. That would have been the smart play. You thought too small and screwed yourself with the Machine and with the Family. Quite an accomplishment, really — "

"Maybe we should tie you up, after all," Miguel said. "And gag you, too."

The sounds of several car doors slamming reached us from the front of the house.

"Hands!" Miguel ordered. "Go greet our guests so we can settle this."

"Too late," Jesus said. "Told you. You're already so fucked you're bowlegged. Give it … less than a minute now."

Miguel chuckled but I know a hollow laugh when I hear it. Miguel was a terrible poker player. He thought he had a hot hand. Maybe so, but his heart wasn't cold enough.

T here was a squawking sound. It sounded like Hands, but it was Hands making sounds strained through a tight grip around his throat.

"Bruder?" Jesus lowered his sunglasses and looked up at Miguel's thug. "Hey, brother. Time for some fast life or death decisions on your part. You got two cartridges in that weapon. Good for quail, sweeping an alley and great for the front gate. Lousy choice for this situation."

Bruder grimaced at Jesus.

"They'll be coming in through that gate on the other side of the pool. You should have gone for heavier ordnance, dude. I suppose you could shoot yourself and maybe Hands. That would save some time and a few rounds."

The thug glowered at Jesus and pointed the shotgun his way.

Jesus just shook his head. "If I were you, I'd shoot *these* assholes." He pointed at Miguel and International Mel. "Denny and I would appreciate the gesture. That looks to me like the only way you get out of this alive. I mean, whatever happens next, you're the goon who goes down first. Miguel pay you enough to get shot and killed? Hard to imagine how much money that would take."

Bruder frowned more as the squawking sound continued and grew louder.

"See, you thought you were in the power position because you have the shotgun," Jesus explained patiently. "I counted four door slams. Denny's coming this way and he's not alone. He's Godzilla over Tokyo. He's Vader taking the lightsaber to the younglings in the Jedi temple. He's Big Bad Voodoo Daddy. Denny's the guy who took over the whole Machine. You think he's going to come in here like a gentleman and pay for what's his? The head of the Machine doesn't ask. He tells. Your boss made a miscalculation when he got greedy and you're about to pay for it. Doesn't seem fair to me."

Bruder growled and I couldn't help but break into a big beaming smile, too. "Perfect!" I enthused. "It's like you're sent over from Central Casting! Look at you, all muscly and German and stuff."

Jesus guffawed. "He's Jaws in the Bond movies, right? He's the big bad guy but if you run for the beach now, you still get to live to fight another day. How about it, big guy? Want a place in the sequels or is this your day to die?"

Miguel looked anxious and, with a trembling hand, waved at Bruder. "Hey! Focus! If Denny comes heavy, shoot the hostages."

He pointed his shotgun at Jesus' head.

Jesus took a sip of his drink and continued to smile up at the big man. "Hey, I'm just sitting here with a mojito watching Miguel's gamble play out. Looks to me like your boss has left you holding a shit hand, man. Underestimating the enemy. *Classic* fuck-up. Too common."

Bruder brought the muzzle closer to Jesus' face. Jesus didn't look at the gun. He watched the big man's face. His gaze was steady. Bruder had begun to sweat heavily.

Jesus stayed cold, just like he told me to be. He couldn't possibly be as relaxed as he appeared. I knew that, but watching him work I wanted to take Jesus to Vegas and see what damage he could do playing Texas hold 'em.

Through the iron gate leading into the backyard, I saw three guys in black suits enter. Each carried a submachine gun.

"Uh-oh," Jesus said. "Way too late."

Behind the trio strode Big Denny De Molina in a grey suit. I hadn't seen Denny since New York. He had Hands by the neck. That must be what took them so long. Hands made the mistake of trying to struggle as Denny walked him backward. As Denny spun the creep around, I saw that Hands' face was bloody. Denny's expensive suit had crimson on the sleeve. I'd known him as an enforcer. Apparently, as a boss, Big Denny hadn't let go of his old role. He was a hands-on micromanager with muscle under all that fat.

Miguel left us to stand beside the pool and try to calm the situation. International Mel went with him but stood behind Miguel, perhaps ready to use him as a human shield.

"As one hired gun to another," Jesus told Bruder, "I know you're just doing your job. I know you've had it sweet here, too, but Miguel's checks and chicks don't matter when you're dead. Seconds left. Was there anything you wanted to do or say before you die in a hail of gunfire?"

"No," the big guy said.

"Good. So how about you walk away and let us handle this? You can't possibly be paid enough to deal with this horse shit. It's not worth getting shot in the crotch and bleeding out slowly. Let me take care of this for you."

Bruder said nothing. Instead, he turned, and walked away with his hands in the air, shotgun held high. He headed for the rear gate that led toward the beach.

For a second, I caught the surprise in Jesus' eyes. I whispered, "You should have been a lawyer."

"I took a course in hostage negotiation in the Army. This was my first one." Jesus pushed his sunglasses back up his nose and rose from his lounge chair. He whispered back, "I really didn't think that would work. I was gonna grab the shotgun and probably get shot in the process. I planned to stab the big lug in the throat with the knife in my sock."

"Oh," I said. "Well, that probably wouldn't have gone well."

"Definitely not."

I got up. "Shit, I thought you had this mess locked down and under control."

"Nah, that was just dying breath, romantic-gesture-type desperation. I wanted to look cool for you on the way out."

Jesus wasn't the only one who was surprised. International Mel looked back to see Bruder disappear out of the back gate. Jesus ran then, only dipping a second to grab his blade. Then he had the switchblade against Mel's throat.

Jesus spun the Family's man around and pushed him a few steps toward the pool. Jesus had a human shield and I stood behind my man wishing I had *Abuela's* Walther. The only weapon at hand was the tall mojito glass so I held on to it.

Miguel froze and looked back and forth from Jesus and Mel to Big Denny and his three soldiers. That reminded me of why I left Miguel. He wasn't as smart as he thought he was. He couldn't possibly be as smart as he thought he was.

Jesus waved to Denny across the pool. "Hey, Den! Tell your guys to stay cool while I take care of business, will ya? There's not going to be an auction so everyone can relax."

Jesus barked at Miguel to sit down. "International Mel is valuable to your business and to the Family. Keep him healthy. Sit!"

Miguel sat in a nearby lounge chair.

"Good dog. Lily, get the thing."

I stepped towards Miguel.

He muttered, "Bitch!" as he reached for me.

I broke the mojito glass over his head and he started bleeding and shrieking.

"Dude!" Jesus called to Miguel. "I've got steel on International Mel over here! What were you thinking? You guys are going to have a very awkward Thanksgiving dinner when the Family gets together this year."

I put the jagged edge of my glass to Miguel's neck and he stopped his screaming. Blood ran down his face from his lacerated scalp. My right hand was bloody but if I needed stitches, that would have to wait until I found out if I survived the afternoon.

Miguel had the eyes of a shark. You could scream at him and he wouldn't flinch. He'd argue about things, but problems didn't seem to bother him like they did ordinary people. Miguel didn't care enough to feel any criticism. There was a human element missing — typical serial killer lack of empathy. However, when I told him, "I am so embarrassed I ever slept with you," by his eyes, I think I hurt him for the first time.

Miguel looked in my eyes and saw his death there. He said nothing as he handed me the memory stick.

International Mel started to sputter a threat so Jesus let him feel the blade's edge. A trickle of blood reached down the Family man's throat and he wisely shut his grill.

"*Amigos! Cómo estás?* Hey, Denny! Long time, no see! You look like you've lost weight. Did you lose a pound or is it two?"

Big Denny De Molina's face clouded. "This fucker told us to give up our guns at the gate. Do I look like I'm playin'?" He hit Hands across the face with two vicious bitch slaps before he let Miguel's man go. Then he appeared to think better of it and grabbed Hands and spun him around again so they were face to face. Denny grabbed him by the neck again and squeezed.

I assumed Hands was about to be strangled to death. Instead, the Machine's boss kneed him in the groin so hard, Denny's own men flinched. Then Big Denny threw Hands in the deep end of the pool. That's how we found out Hands couldn't swim.

Could this day get any more perfect?

41

Drowning didn't look how I thought it would. Instead of splashing around side-to-side and trying to tread water, there's a lot more up and down than I expected. Hands disappeared under water, flailed and then pushed with the tips of his shoes just enough to barely break the surface of the water again. He gasped and sputtered and then went down again.

"We got a situation here, but we better keep this short," Jesus told Big Denny. "I've got the stuff you want and Lily's with me. I want to do a deal with you."

Denny stepped to the edge of the pool and crossed his arms. "We already had a deal, Jesus."

Jesus did his best Vader: "Pray I don't change the terms of our agreement again." Jesus did the Darth Vader heavy breathing gag. Hands must have been pretty envious of that right about then.

Denny didn't crack a smile, but a couple of his guys looked at each other and smirked.

"Things got more complex, Denny," Jesus said. "When you sent me after Lily, you told me I was in charge of handling the project. You sent an assassin after her, a whole team, in fact."

Denny looked at me with an unreadable expression. Denny

might have been good at poker, too. No one would know we were all close friends once. "You shoulda found her faster, brother."

Hands broke the surface for the third time. Splashing, he managed to yell, "Help!"

"Shut up," Denny told him. "What do you want, Jesus? What have you got that I don't already have?"

"We keep the skim. You get the inside data on the Machine and this asshole doesn't get it." Jesus tipped his head toward Miguel, still frozen and bleeding on his lounge chair. Of all of us, he had the most to fear. What if he died and had to spend eternity as a ghost in a Speedo and green Crocs?

"The Family wants something on the Machine. If they move into your territory, it'll cost you a lot more than the skim."

Denny glanced at his guys and their submachine guns. "So what?"

"So Lily and I go free, we call a truce and everybody stays in their lane. No unfortunate accidents or incidents."

Denny stared at Jesus across the pool. "And why don't I kill you all right now?"

"Because if International Mel dies, you'll kick off a war with the Family. The Machine isn't up to going to the mattresses, man."

Denny took a moment to watch the drowning man before he gave a slow nod. "Fine."

"I'm disappointed," Jesus said. "When you asked why you shouldn't kill me, I wanted to say, 'You're a daisy if you do!' That was such a great line."

"*Tombstone*. Val fucking Kilmer. Genius!" When Denny smiled at that, I understood why he and Jesus had once been such great friends.

"How many times did we see that movie, Denny?"

A bigger smile spread across Denny's face. "A lot."

"With Kurt fucking Russell!" Jesus said. "We had good times, Den. A lot of history."

"Yeah." Denny turned to his guys and motioned for them to lower their weapons. "Somebody better pull that fool out of the pool, for peace with the Family."

Jesus smiled. "I'll be your huckleberry." He glanced at me and gave me a wink.

The deal seemed to fall into place. My shoulders loosened a little as the tension eased. "Fuckin' A!"

We were going to live and run off to French Polynesia. I was going to be free of the Machine's bullshit...of *any* bullshit.

Then Bruder smashed out an upstairs window and began firing on Denny's men. I should have known Bruder's retreat was too good to be true. He'd taken at least some of Jesus' advice to heart. However, instead of walking away, the big thug must have circled back to the house from the beach to retrieve a better weapon.

Bruder rained steel down on Denny's entourage with the familiar chatter of an AK-47. He had an elevated position and much better firepower and he wasn't running away.

I think the expression that applies here is: My heart was in my mouth. Or it could be a wicked case of acid reflux. Seconds to live can bring that on.

42

Bruder peppered two of the guys from the Machine and killed them in his first few bursts. As Denny ran to the corner of the house by the entrance to the rear of the mountain, the third soldier kept Bruder occupied. Miguel's thug wounded that third man in the leg.

The wounded man, his hair bleached so impossibly blond his head was almost white, didn't just drop his weapon. He fell backward into a huge terracotta clay pot, ass first. In rapid Spanish, he screamed uselessly to his dead buddies for help.

A lot can happen in a few seconds. None of it made sense in the present tense. It was all senseless violence in the moment. If you survive, you get to go backward and try to make sense of it. Figuring out what's happening when you see everything through an adrenaline-drenched lens feels like trying to put a shattered vase back together while all the little pieces are still bouncing off the floor and skittering under the couch.

Funny how the big scary moments have a way of splitting time. Events happen fast, but nothing seems sequential anymore. Your brain takes it all in, breaks it into pieces, slows it down and shakes it up so it is an indistinct whole. When you try to break a disaster down, it can never capture the energy of everything happening at once. Split-second choices are made that maybe aren't really choices. Instead, they're just reactions that occur, things to trip over along the path, inevitable.

Afterward, someone would try to pick apart our sins — detectives, forensic specialists, a judge and jury, God. All that Monday morning quarterbacking and 20/20 hindsight couldn't take into account the fact that nobody's thinking straight when shit goes sideways and the brake and the accelerator in your brain are pushed to the floor at the same time.

It's as if someone had written a script and we're all just playing out the action. Every frame of this hyperreality was filmed in brighter pastel as our overloaded brains tried to soak it all in. Hyperreality, ironically, didn't feel real.

I think I understood then something Jesus had tried to explain to me: If you pretend you're the star in the movie of your life, you feel safer from death. There's always the chance of a sequel. Pretending what happened next in a film was what got me through it.

Action!

International Mel Fordman was wearing that stupid bullet-resistant suit. Jesus' blade was already at his throat so that fancy suit didn't protect him from the cut. Maybe it was shock at the sudden gunfire, maybe mercy, but Jesus let go of his human shield.

The knife wound at Mel's neck was just a nick. In his panic, he must have thought his carotid artery was slit. He screamed and stumbled at the pool's edge, then tumbled in headfirst.

Between the armor in his heavy suit and fear shutting his brain down, I didn't think of Mel as a murder victim. He was more like a Darwin award winner. International Mel would have survived but Hands was so busy trying not to die, he assured Mel's death. The creep did what drowning people do. Hands latched onto Mel in a death grip and wouldn't let go. They drowned together.

Maybe Mel died of a heart attack and drowning. Either way, Jesus did warn him that, by disrespecting me, he'd have to die horribly. That was one package delivered to Hell.

Jesus grabbed me and we started for the rear gate that led to the beach. Bruder saw that move and cut off our escape with a few shots in the dirt in front of us. He might have shot us but Miguel was right on our heels and I guessed Bruder didn't want to shoot his boss. After this, he'd be looking for a big bonus and a vacation in Mexico.

Jesus, Miguel and I backed up, pinned until the gunfire between the Family and Machine ran its course.

Despite his wound and initial shock at getting hit, Denny's bleached blond soldier had gathered his faculties. He looked like he knew what he was doing. He hugged the base of the water fountain as he changed mags. Meanwhile, Bruder chewed up the garden and wooden fence around him with slugs from the chattering AK.

Blondie waited for Bruder to change mags before opening up from cover. He didn't make the mistake of aiming. He only poked his weapon out and fired in the big thug's general direction. Wisely, he wasn't looking to strike Bruder out with this weapon. His was suppressing fire, meant to brush Bruder back from the plate.

Bruder was not an idiot, either. He didn't stand in the middle of the shattered window frame waiting to get shot. He pulled back to change mags. This back and forth would go on for a while.

Maybe Bruder hoped the Machine's man would try to advance on him, bleed out or run out of ammo. Blondie didn't take the bait.

My teeth hurt from clenching my jaw so hard. Following Jesus' example, I'd often wished for a life that echoed a movie. I should have been more specific. I should have wished for a Julie Andrews film (or at least one of those porn movies geared to female audiences).

Somewhere up the beach in another fancy mansion, I imagined Yanni was having tea and wondering vaguely what the fuck the commotion at the neighbor's house was all about. I wondered if he was picking up the phone, calling the LEOs and hoping they'd sort it out so he could get back to writing some calming music.

Meanwhile, the guy behind the water fountain screamed to Denny. If I were him, I would have tried playing dead despite the searing pain. His best hope was for Bruder to ignore him, or at least decide to save the ammunition and let him bleed out.

In any case, Denny didn't answer. I couldn't see where the Machine's boss had got off to. In a moment, I had my answer. Denny must have gotten into the house to flank Bruder. A pistol barked twice and the big German slumped in the open window, alive but not for long.

I got busy running. Jesus and I reached for each other. No plan. No strategy. I just knew I had a better shot at living if I stuck with him. I hoped he felt the same.

Big Denny appeared in the upstairs window and drew a bead on me.

When I knew him, Denny could be sweet. Those days were gone. As head of the Machine, he was all about what needed to be done, what earned and what stood in the way of earning.

Denny peered out to fire shots our way. He raised a nickel-plated .38 that, to me, looked like the center of the fucking universe. (What is it about nickel plated .38s? The guys with money just seem to love them while Glocks are for everybody else.) He screamed something I couldn't make out over the gunfire. He probably wasn't yelling, "Happy birthday!" or "There's a sale at Macy's!" His man behind the water fountain still wasn't looking at his target so he kept throwing shots blindly. The suppressing fire hit the back of the house not far from Denny.

Denny threw shots our way and screamed some more but, in the end, it was all just vowel sounds carrying inarticulate rage.

I didn't know if Big Denny meant to hit Miguel, but he did. Miguel was two steps behind me when he got shot in the belly. No amount of sit-ups and planking in Pilates class stops a slug. The path of the bullet opened Miguel's gut like a piñata spilling candy.

In a few moments, Miguel would look like he was sitting by the pool in red Bermuda shorts. At least all that gore covered up the Speedo. What galactic level of narcissism possesses a grown man who isn't gay and on the Riviera to wear a French-cut Speedo?

It turned out it was impossible to run at full speed and keep low at the same time. I actually hit my right cheek with my right knee trying to get the fuck out of there. I staggered as Jesus pulled me toward the back gate.

With one last look, I got an eyeful of Miguel writhing as he turned inside out: lots of guts, followed by spurting and oozing.

Miguel looked my way and I felt bad for him. I forgave him for the green Crocs.

Am I not merciful?

43

A s Jesus and I sprinted down the path to the beach, I considered a new possibility seriously: Maybe working as a barista at Starbucks wouldn't be so bad. Maybe French Polynesia has a rainy season that makes everything moldy. Maybe poisonous spiders as big as hands live in the mattresses of those beautiful resorts. Maybe the wi-fi really sucks.

I found myself wondering how much dental hygienists make in a year and what's the vacation package like? Maybe taking the blue pill and remaining another useful pawn in *The Matrix* is the sane choice. Waking up among the normal ordinaries isn't all winning but most people don't have to lose this hard either.

The dead guys in Miguel's backyard had names before they painted the pretty scenery in pink mist and crimson gore. They had friends, probably. Even assholes have friends. Maybe the two corpses in the grass were best buds.

A few minutes ago, they were tough guys with guns. A few years before that, their biggest problems were trying to pass algebra and failing to get the go-ahead to slip a hand under their first girlfriend's bra. Go back further and they were peaceful little babies. Once upon a time, their mothers and fathers looked down into a crib and thought to themselves, *This kid! Sucking his thumb! Look how perfect he is! He could be anything! He could be President. He could be an astronaut. He could change the world. His name could be spoken for generations with respect and we're part of that glorious legacy because we made love and we made him!*

Smash cut to reality: They had become meat. Worse, they were bit players, expendable and forgotten while trying to fulfill someone else's dreams of wealth and power.

A few dozen bad choices and happenstance I'll never know led them to an early death. One good choice might have put them somewhere else. *Sorry! So long, dead thugs!*

No wonder Jesus preferred movies to real life. Real life was messy as fuck. Hollywood promises order and happy endings. Much better to keep pretending and keep our film moving forward.

I didn't want to be a barista putting up with rude customers. I didn't want to be a dental hygienist living for a couple of weeks off a year but stuck with staycations because the pay really wasn't that good. And if French Polynesia had big spiders and the rainy season lasted too long, I'd set spider traps and buy a sun lamp.

The truth was, I'd made lots of bad choices. I didn't want to rethink my million little choices that had led me to that day. I wanted to live large. That meant a high risk of dying young.

Hundreds of thousands of corporate offices, staff rooms and conference halls across America displayed bullshit motivational posters about going for the brass ring, hanging in there, taking risks and persevering. Ordinary citizens had to put up with useless meetings, icebreakers and team-building exercises. They drank stale coffee from mugs espousing empty slogans like, "No guts, no glory."

Maybe it was the adrenaline of surviving gunfire that clouded my brain but it occurred to me that mob life, though full of deception, was very low on bullshit. There was no room for empty slogans and small aspirations when you're facing down bad men with guns.

Chests heaving and starved for air, Jesus and I paused on the hot sand. "Lily? You okay?"

"The espresso is better on my side of the American dream," I said. "And there's no uniforms or stupid mugs with pictures of aspiring cats on them."

"Huh?"

"I'm fine," I panted. "On with our action movie: third reel. What's next?"

"We've got to do something dumb."

"I'm in!"

"We've got to double back."

"Oh. Well, shit."

"Yeah."

44

B ig Denny had come heavy. Two black SUVs sat in Miguel's
driveway, engines still cooking. "That's not very environ-
mentally sound," Jesus said.

"Black SUVs are kinda cliche, aren't they?"

Jesus slid me a smile. "The FBI and the mob mirror each other
in that way."

We were both still shaking from nearly being killed, but that was
okay as long as we weren't bleeding from essential organs. We
pretended the carnage didn't bother us but we weren't fooling each
other. To be caught in the middle of a shooting gallery without
serious weaponry was terrifying.

My right hand was still bleeding from the broken mojito glass.
When I got a moment, I planned to pick the glass out of it. The
wound stung like a wasp but the damage was superficial.

"Let's take one of the SUVs," I told Jesus. "You get our stuff
from the rental. I'll look in the gatehouse and get the gate open.

Jesus stayed with the second SUV for a moment as I wheeled
over to the gate. I assumed he was looking for weapons or ammo.

The little gatehouse was tucked to one side of the gate. It held
one small unlocked cabinet. Besides a case of Pepsi and a few

bags of Doritos, I found our cell phones, Jesus' SIG and my Walther.

Jesus caught up with me and took his SIG and phone with a smile. "You look worried."

"I can't imagine why. Let's get out of here before Denny comes out with his soldier."

"Denny's slow and his guy is wounded. He's probably still clearing the house or looking for us on the beach, but yeah, let's go. Everything is coming up Jesus and Lily again."

I pushed a button on the wall and the gate began to slide open. We were about to get back in the SUV and haul ass when more chatter rose from the mansion's front door. Jesus yanked me backward by my hair and pulled me to cover behind the engine block.

"Ouch." I rubbed my scalp, but it wasn't the roots of my hair that bothered me. I swear I'd felt the wind of a round splitting the air an inch from my face.

"Sorry," he said.

I was the one who was sorry. In my hurry to get our weapons from the gatehouse, I parked at a bad angle. Denny could take us out no matter how we tried to get back into the SUV.

"How long before the cops show up, do you think?" I ask.

"Can't be long now."

"How long has it been already?"

"A few minutes."

"Feels like hours," I said.

"Time will slow down in jail."

"We should have just run down the beach and left the weapons."

"We need to get some distance from this place. If we'd run down the beach or the road, someone would catch up with us. If we're lucky, whoever finds us will only want to arrest us."

"I don't want to get arrested or shot by cops in Yanni's backyard," I said, "but staying here isn't the best option, either. Shall we just wait for the local sheriff to come out with a bunch of deputies and start shooting back?"

It wasn't a serious question. We'd be caught in the middle. Our odds of surviving were draining away by the second.

"Denny's got an AK-47. We've got pistols," Jesus said. At this distance, he had little to worry about from us. I found myself staring at the patch of driveway between us and the open gate. I pictured myself running for freedom and feeling the target in the middle of my back. I imagined myself almost making it and, just as I'm about to step back into cover, Denny would nail me in the spine with three rounds. I could already see myself bleeding out on that hot patch of driveway. It wasn't a pretty picture.

"Denny!" Jesus called. "Let's talk!"

"You talk too much!" Denny fired again, pitting the St. Augustine grass just a few feet away from where we cowered.

"He's going to get his fat ass out of that doorway and come at us any minute," I said. "He'll get us with the AK before we have a chance to hit him with what we've got."

Jesus nodded. "Yeah, we could hurt him but not before he killed us."

Then we heard distant sirens.

Jesus leaned close and kissed my cheek. He whispered, "Salvation."

"**G**et ready to move," Jesus told me. "We'll both go in the passenger side. You're first, you drive. I'll fire on him to keep him back."

I didn't usually take orders, but I was okay with making an exception when there were no other choices.

Just then, Denny's wounded man, the bleached blond, limped through the gate from the back of the mansion. In obvious pain, he came up along the corner of the house. "B.D.!" he called to his boss. "It's me!"

Encouraged to have reinforcement, Denny emerged from the doorway and I knew we'd waited too long to run.

Salvation came in a surprising form. It wasn't the cops who would break up the pool party. It was Bruder. The big German lurched out of the doorway behind Denny, bleeding but still armed.

Denny was focused on our position. As the blond guy rounded the corner, he spotted Bruder staggering up behind his boss. In a panic, Blondie raised his submachine gun and fired off a few rounds that missed Denny and Bruder. Chunks and splinters of wood sprayed from a pillar between them.

The siren's wail was getting closer and I guessed that Miguel's cozy and relaxed relationship with Manalapan's incurious LEOs wouldn't survive his death.

Denny had fallen down the steps and was staying down, looking back toward the house, searching for a target. The blond merc shattered some windows with another few rounds. That accomplished little but did drive Bruder to stagger back inside the mansion's front door.

As soon as he got to cover, Bruder opened up again with a little pistol that went *pop, pop, pop!*

"Feels like our last dance," I said.

"Oh, ye of little faith," Jesus replied.

I punched his shoulder with my injured hand. *Worth it.*

Bruder paused to change mags. Denny got up and ran for his SUV. He fired his weapon toward the front door as he went.

Blondie limped as fast as he could to the same truck. He got behind the engine block and was in a much better position to strafe the mansion.

Meanwhile, Denny was screaming at him, "Get in the car! Get in the car, you dumb sonofabitch!"

We took the hint and ran for the SUV I'd chosen. Blondie could have turned and shot us but our truck was blocking the gate. Killing us meant trapping themselves between Bruder and Manapalan's police department.

As we got in and roared off, I heard Big Denny De Molina scream, "*Jesus!* Jesus Diaz! *Bastardo!*"

I expected the back window to shatter in a hail of gunfire, like in the movies. Instead, we pulled out and there wasn't a cop or an assassin from the Machine in sight. As soon as I straightened out, I spotted cruisers in my rearview mirror.

"Don't speed," Jesus advises.

"I know."

The cop cars turned into Miguel's mansion in a cloud of hot dust, sirens howling and lights blazing. None of them followed us.

"Did you hear Denny yelling?"

"I did," Jesus said. He held up a ring of car keys and twirled it on his index finger. "I think he wanted help finding these." He tossed the keys to Denny's SUV out of the open window.

I couldn't help it. I chuckled and I cried at the same time. All the shock of the events of the last few minutes began to wear off. We were safe enough so we didn't have to pretend to be cool anymore.

Jesus chuckled and shook, too. "Like the pilots say, 'Any landing you walk away from is a good landing.'"

It's a nice thought, but I was sobering up a little too fast from the high of facing death and surviving. "This isn't over, though, is it?"

"Not by a long shot," Jesus replied. "Back in the day, he'd be fucked but Denny's got big money behind him now. He'll surrender and so will his boy. They'll spin some tale of self-defense, maybe. I don't know but he'll tell the DA some story about how he got caught in the middle of one of those violent disputes Florida is infamous for. The cops will know that's bullshit but lawyers are different from cops. Nothing's black and white with them. He's got money. They'll swing bail for Denny somehow. Then he'll probably jump bail and be back in New York soon."

"You're exaggerating, right?"

"*Mm*...maybe not soon but soon enough. Our central problem hasn't changed just because Denny's in the can and inconvenienced for a bit." Jesus shrugged. "What are you gonna do? American justice. It's made for guys with big money and sharp lawyers."

"Denny is a real businessman now. I wish I was that untouchable."

One thing about growing up inside the Machine, I felt safe (especially after I shot Carmine and my parents got rid of him). I missed that feeling. Nothing could touch me then, at least not until a power play inside the Spanish mob nearly brought it down.

I pulled over at a wide spot in the road and punched Jesus as hard as I could with my good hand. I punctuated every syllable of the following sentence with a punch to his chest. "Why did you not kill Denny when you had the chance?" Punching Jesus with my left made me forget the pain in my right.

"Ease off," Jesus said.

"Why should I?"

"If you stop hitting me, I'll tell you how we're going to get away."

I stopped. "You have a plan?"

"Plan? That's a little grandiose. I have an idea. Since we ran into and over Ortega at that mall, we're too hot. With all that surveillance, the airports are probably a trap no matter how many pamphlets about Hello Kitty I have in my luggage."

I settled back in my seat and restarted the engine.

"We're headed back to New York, aren't we?" I said.

"We'll have to drive."

I leaned over and gave Jesus a sweet, soft kiss. Then I punched him in the gut one more time when he wasn't expecting it, just for good measure.

"Florida's too hot for us," I said. "Let's get on the road."

46

It was six hours to Savannah and I don't think I took a full breath until we crossed into Georgia. We found a motel to hole up.

Jesus dealt with the clerk at the front desk. As soon as he came out, we exchanged keys and he took the SUV to dump it somewhere far away. I made the long slog to our room. The place was a dump. Ugly pictures of alligators were screwed to the walls. I imagine they were meant to be cute.

I took a long shower. To my surprise, by the time I came out, Jesus was back with coffee and supplies to clean and bandage my wounds. He changed the bandage on my forearm where Cherry skinned me a little, too.

He was careful to make sure all the glass was out before he hit my fist with the anti-bacterial spray. That stung like a bitch. Head wounds bleed most. Hand and gut wounds hurt the most. I wished I didn't know this shit so well.

"If this were an old Bond movie, I'd get away with barely a scratch," I said.

Jesus frowned and shook his head. "If this were an old Bond

movie, you'd be painted gold and drowned inside a waterbed or something."

"Drowned inside a waterbed? That makes no sense."

He shrugged. "Evens out. If this were a new Bond movie, I'd be tortured more. Since Christopher Nolan made Batman movies edgy and dark, Hollywood only has one mood. They try to make everything look more realistic. Unfortunately, that makes a lot of those stories less fun."

"Wait a minute!" I said. "You think you're the Bond? I'm the Bond in this flick. You're like the...snarky film critic guy or something."

Jesus chuckled as he finished wrapping my hand. When he was done, he raised my hand to his lips and gave it the lightest of kisses. "All better."

"Not all better."

"Soon, Mrs. Bond. In the meantime, I had some new thoughts on the subject of our big getaway. I made some moves."

"Moves? Without talking to me first?"

"I called Marco," he said.

"Who?"'

"My connection to the Family. He couldn't help me, but he put me in touch with a guy named Billy."

"Who's Billy?"

"One of Miguel's pilots. International Mel gave me the idea. They move shit across the border all the time."

"I'm thinking we stick with the plan, get back to New York and settle this once and forever with Denny. Beats spending the rest of my life running. What are you thinking?" I asked.

"Denny took shots at us. We owe the Machine nothing. Suppose we get a plane ride from Billy? How would you like to go to Honduras via Narco Airlines? From there, I think we should check out Uruguay."

"Let me guess," I said. "The price of airfare is the memory stick. The Family will use it to take over the Machine's territory. They'll have a huge chunk of all the Spanish mob's biz in NYC. We'll be rats."

"We'll be live rats. If Denny had acted civilized, we wouldn't be doing any of this shit and everybody could have walked away happy."

"Well, Denny would not have been happy — "

"Compromise," Jesus said, "is where everybody gets what they need but nobody gets what they want. If everybody's just about equally pissed, that's a good deal, right? Denny didn't want to do that. He wanted the whole pie. Now, he's got real trouble. He's smart, but he's not smart enough to deescalate. Assholes are always making a bad day worse."

"And some asshole started making moves without me. To solve problems," I said, "I don't ask what Jesus would do. I ask what my mother would do. Mom wouldn't run. She'd attack."

"Jesus wept," Jesus said. But Jesus Diaz didn't weep. He just sighed heavily. "How is your Mom? She take over the Devil's throne in Hell yet?"

"You never liked my Mom."

"She never liked me."

"Truth."

"Let's put a pin in this and give me time to think about more options. Going to war is not the best option. There are only two of us."

"If my mom's on board, that would make us twenty-five or so."

I stripped the duvet from the motel bed because the possibility of bed bugs and the certainty of old semen creeped me out. Then I lay back on the motel bed to do some serious worrying.

Jesus sat on the edge of the bed and rubbed my feet. "Relax. It's a good deal for us and for the Family."

"You don't think the Family will be pissed at us for Miguel and Hands and International Mel being inconveniently gutted and drowned and all? Bruder is shot and probably dead. I don't think anyone will miss him at the next cotillion. He wasn't much of a conversationalist, but still — "

"I told Billy every bit of that was Denny's doing. Besides, Billy's just got a field promotion now that Mel and Miguel are dead. Pulling us out of the shit will be his first official act as a transit boss. He'll want this to go smooth."

"What are we going to do in Uruguay?"

"I figured we'd live on love for a while."

"We'll get hungry."

"You've got enough cash for a while, right?"

"You plan to live off me? Be a kept man?"

"I figured I'd be your bodyguard."

"Got any experience?"

"I'll shoot you a resume as soon as I get around to it. I was thinking there's a lot of money to be made investing in marijuana dispensaries. Colorado is nice, especially in the summer. California is nice all the time. Canada's gotten on the legalization bandwagon, too. How about we pick up some stocks and live off the dividends?"

"I dunno. I don't know anything about Uruguay. What happened to French Polynesia?"

"Make enough in the weed business and you can buy French Polynesia."

"I don't know."

"There are lots of options, Lily. We don't have to decide what to do with the rest of our lives this second. All we have to do is get out of here clean and cool. The Family will kill Denny and the Machine will fall apart. Things will settle down immensely. All anybody wants to do is to be left alone to make money. Even the lowest soldiers know that so it's fall in line and make money or die. The more they run their deals quietly, the more money they get. Mob wars suck up resources and are bad for business. You watch. Give it a little time, and neither of us will have to go around strapped and armed for bear all the time."

I took a deep breath and let the air hiss out between my teeth. The foot massage felt good. I was softening, willing to put off until tomorrow what I could worry endlessly about today. "What's the plan for tonight?"

"There's a couple of places around the corner. I'll slip out and get us a bucket of chicken."

"*Ick.*"

"Hey, I came up with a new rule for myself. Any day somebody shoots bullets in my direction, I get to have Kentucky Fried Chicken. As long as I survive, it's okay. We dodged death today. We deserve it."

"As long as we don't get shot at all the time, I guess it's okay."

"How about we stay in tonight? I'll rent us a movie."

"If you say *Thelma and Louise*, I'm going to punch you in the gut again."

"Let's watch something fun and light. I was thinking *Butch Cassidy and the Sundance Kid*. It's written by William Goldman. Everybody thinks of *The Princess Bride* when they hear William Goldman, but all his movies have great dialogue. It's funny stuff. You'll love it. Two outlaws, living by their wits — "

"Which one am I?" I asked. "Butch or Sundance?"

"I guess you're more of a Sundance."

"I like the sound of that."

It turned out, I did love the movie. Paul Newman and Robert Redford tore it up. The back and forth was funny and the bike riding montage to the song *Raindrops Keep Falling On My Head* was a brilliant, unexpected choice. It was awesome, right up until Butch and Sundance made a hopeless stand and died in a hail of gunfire.

"Shit, Jesus!"

As the credits rolled, he said, "In case things don't go according to plan tomorrow, we should figure out a place for us to meet up. In case we get separated."

I said nothing and Jesus whispered, "Sorry about the movie. I guess I was remembering all the fun stuff."

"I have a better memory for all the bad stuff."

"I'll keep you safe, Lily."

"And I'll keep you safe, Jesus."

"What happened to Butch and Sundance won't happen to us," he said.

"Promise?"

"Promise. Lots of people are after us but the Bolivian military has absolutely no interest in getting in a shoot-out — "

I punched him in the gut with my good hand again.

Jesus and I didn't make love that night. We hardly talked, either. I was the little spoon and he was the big spoon and he held me tight a long time before we fell asleep.

When I woke up in the morning, my head was still on Jesus' arm. At his wrist, poking out at the edge of his sleeve, was the handle of a knife. That was new. Even in sleep, he had a weapon on him. Jesus was a weapon.

We have to stop living like this, I thought.

The trick was to keep living long enough to figure out how to be safe. I decided Jesus was right. The smarter move was not to run back to New York and into the war zone between the Machine and the Family.

B illy turned out to be an older man in a blue leisure suit. I didn't know they still made leisure suits. His salt and pepper hair was a flat top and the sides of his head were shaved tight. He pulled up in an old station wagon. A cloud of dust and burning oil hung behind the chugging vehicle.

Jesus and I circled Billy's car. Jesus was probably checking the back seat for ninjas. I was distracted by Billy's ride. The wagon was so old, it had wood paneling down the sides. The ass end was plastered with bumper stickers on top of bumper stickers. Most of them were election stickers. One, barely readable, read: *Clinton will have us all on our knees.* I assumed that was a Slick Willie blowjob joke, not a Hillary joke.

There was also a faded *Baby on board* and *I love my wiener dog!* Another bumper sticker proclaimed: *More Bush, Less Gore!* I wasn't sure if that was a dated political statement or a call for more porn and less violence.

"How do you keep this thing running?" I asked.

Billy smiled. "The Chevy Caprice is an American classic! There's still Tin Lizzies on the road. You don't think I can keep this old woody wagon going?"

"Nice stickers," Jesus observed.

"You think they're stupid. You're thinking I'm stupid."

"No, no," I said, maybe a little too quickly and too loudly.

Billy gave me a stern look. "Lily, if we're going to get along, you gotta tell the truth, okay?"

"I don't think they're stupid. They're...interesting."

"I know what interesting means, *chica*. I call this ride my stealth wagon. I got a radar detector up front and a bunch of bumper stickers on the back. This is *Georgia*. I'm *invisible* to cops all the way down to the panhandle. The DEA is always looking above the radar. This wagon and this haircut puts me way below the radar. Trust me, I know. I'm a pilot."

Jesus shrugged. "Low profile. We get it. Should fix it so it doesn't burn so much oil, though. That's a lot of white smoke."

Billy grunted and barreled on. "You want to know what I spend my money on?"

I wasn't going to guess cars, clothes or hair stylists.

Billy didn't wait for us to answer, anyway. "Floatation tanks. Started out as a side gig to launder money. It's getting to be a solid, legit gig on its own. I do a little weed and I float every night. Puts things in perspective. Gettin' in the tank with a couple of tons of salt gives you such buoyancy. It's like floating in space. No gravity gets you, whatsoever. Clears the mind and your body soaks up the minerals ... magnesium or some shit. Keeps the muscles loose and relaxed. You should try it."

"The floatation tank business must be good. You'd have a lot of money to hide," Jesus said.

Billy laughed. "You know what the Family spends money on? Boats and planes. Everybody's jonesing for another hit. Despite all the talk of border security, the Family supplies America's demand for high grade South American recreational pharmaceuticals."

I tried to remember the last time I heard the word *jonesing*. I couldn't. Billy had obviously been in the game a long time. That was oddly reassuring. If the Family had sent a younger guy, I'd be more nervous. An older emissary suggested to me this run was safe. Billy was valuable to the Family so our deal was important to them.

We climbed in the back of the station wagon and roared off.

"How far to the airfield?" Jesus asked.

"Not far," Billy said, "but there's time enough to talk. Tell me again what happened at Miguel's place."

"We were in the middle of making the deal when the cops showed up," Jesus said. It was a lie, of course, but it kept Jesus and me as far away from blame as possible.

"Hands and Bruder are dead," Billy said.

"We saw International Mel fall in Miguel's pool," I volunteered.

"Mel was an asshole," Billy said. "He was my boss for years. I should have been his boss. Higher up, they thought Mel had style. I'm the one who knows my way around a spreadsheet. I was always making Mel look good. He never gave me any credit. He will not be missed. Too bad he drowned. I was hoping Mel would die in a fire, the prick!"

I looked at Jesus and I wondered if he was thinking what I was: Whether it's office politics or mafia business, high school never ends. Somebody's always up and trying to keep somebody else down.

I was looking forward to getting on Billy's plane and opting out. It would just be Jesus and me, no hierarchy. We'd be king and queen of our own prom. We'd never deal with the thousand little insults to dignity that begin when most people wake up in the morning and end only when they pass out from exhaustion or die.

People say we get shorter in old age because the disks in our spines dry out. That's not it. We get shorter due to the weight of responsibilities we carry on our shoulders and the crushing burden of regret in our heads. In short: Adulting sucks.

Juicing greens is not the fountain of youth. A good diet and exercise doesn't keep people happy and looking young. Only having excess money on hand can do that.

"You've got the item we need?" Billy asked. "No bullshit?"

I nodded. The memory stick was in my purse.

Billy nodded and said nothing for a few miles. Traffic was heavy and eighteen-wheelers roared past us. Billy stuck to the speed limit and I began to relax a little, settling back in my seat and holding hands with Jesus.

I wondered if I'd ever come back to America. I'd wanted to see New Orleans during Mardi Gras but never got around to it. The arch in St. Louis looked kind of cool, too. And, of course, I loved New York. Maybe I'd come back for a visit but not before all my hair had turned gray.

Suddenly, I wasn't relaxed, anymore. I was almost weepy. I'd never see my mother again. I stared out of the window and pretended the traffic was fascinating.

We ended up on a two-lane strip of broken road. The Atlantic spread out to our right. Tiny motels held together loosely by peeling paint, and tourist traps full of cheap souvenirs, and sunglass huts dotted the roadsides.

Occasionally, I saw people on the beach, but no one was in the water. A stench reached us.

"Red tide!" Billy told us. "I feel bad for the tourists. They come down here for a week on the beach. They get that fart smell instead. Sad."

I was relieved when Billy turned inland and we got away from that smell of rot.

Billy pulled off onto a dirt road and up to a gate. This wasn't like Miguel's mansion. The industrial fencing stood high and was topped with coils of razor wire.

Our host got out and left the engine chugging as he unlocked the big padlock on the gate.

I leaned on Jesus and put my head on his shoulder. "We're almost free."

Jesus put a hand on the nape of my neck and kissed my forehead. "I've been almost free a few times now. I'll relax after we're in Uruguay, and even then, I probably won't relax for a few weeks."

"Jesus?"

"Yeah?"

"I like you when you're serious. You know that, right?"

"What do you mean?"

"You don't have to try so hard with me. You don't always have to be on. Sometimes I feel like you're performing for me, trying to keep me entertained…trying to be the man. You don't have to try. We're good, okay? I mean…I love you."

He went quiet and when I raised my head to look at him, he smiled. "I love you, too."

As Billy climbed back behind the wheel, Bruder popped the front passenger door open and slid into the passenger seat. He had a revolver in his fist and it was pointed at me. The big German was banged up pretty badly and a bit of blood has seeped through the bandages under his shirt. His torso looked extra bulky from all the bandages beneath that shirt.

"Billy said you were dead," Jesus said.

"I lied," Billy said. "Denny would have killed him if he hadn't been in such a hurry to kill you, Jesus."

Bruder shrugged.

"Well, damn, son!" Jesus exclaimed. "You survived for the sequel after all! You're the last terrorist at the end of *Die Hard*!"

We should have just run down the beach and asked to stay at Yanni's house until the heat died down, I thought. *I could use some of that calming coma music right about now.*

Billy looked back and laughed so hard he revealed several back teeth, black with rot. I guessed he thought spending money on dentists was too modern and flashy.

"Don't you be lookin' so angry, *chica*. I lied about Bruder, but you two lied first. Bruder told me everything about what really went down at Miguel's place."

"I didn't know the ape could talk," I said.

"Get your damn paws off us, you damn dirty ape!" Jesus said.

Billy laughed.

Bruder stared hard at Jesus.

When I was growing up, my father suggested nice girls use their words in an argument. Mom told me the Vasquez girls are more to the point and succinct. I punched my love in the shoulder.

W e rolled up on five rundown buildings that stood in a rough line between the woody wagon and a seaplane tied at the end of a floating pier. As we climbed out of the car, Bruder raised his weapon to kill us. Billy stopped him. "Let them get their luggage out of the trunk. I'm not carrying bags for dead people."

Billy opened the trunk and waved us toward our stuff, but Jesus shook his head.

Billy made a jerk-off motion with one hand and nods toward the trunk.

Jesus stepped forward to stand in front of the open trunk, hands up. He looked at Bruder and smiled. "You know you're only alive because you took my advice. If you had stayed by the pool with that shotgun, no way you would have got out of there. You owe me, Bruder."

Bruder frowned at this, probably because it was true.

"Miguel is dead. Hands is dead and," Jesus looked back at Billy, "International Mel is out of the way. You finally got your promotion. You owe me, man."

"Your people killed ours," Billy said.

"We didn't have 'people,'" I said. "Denny's from the Machine and he tried to kill us, too. You've got the deets on the Spanish mob, the organization, everything."

"The Family doesn't want loose ends," Billy said. "Now shut up!"

"Bruder, you see the injustice here, right?" Jesus persisted. "I saved you and the Family got everything — "

Instead of punching Jesus, Billy slapped me across the mouth. It barely stung. I saw it coming and rolled with it. "That all you got, old man?"

He slapped me again. I saw that coming even before he raised his hand. I rolled with it again. "A little bitch slap only makes bitches cry," I told him.

Stupid guys talk about knowing how to take a punch. By that, they mean, how to endure the pain. I wonder how many punch-drunk idiots who believed the answer to a hard hit was just being tougher. If you're smart and coordinated, "taking a punch" isn't about denying the physics of concussions. It's about getting out of the way, or at least letting your head turn in the direction of the punch. My mother taught me that.

I learned a lot of things hanging out with bad people. I knew what Billy was, for instance. He was one of those guys who smiled as they hit women. His smile was broad but his soul was empty and his gray eyes were cold.

"There's lots of ways to die, Lily," Billy said. "The fast kinds are best. Fuck with me some more, Jesus. I'll show you, starting with her."

Guys like Billy go from sweet kitten to drunk killer jaguar at the flip of a switch. Billy wanted to do something extra terrible. He wanted to make me roll around in the dirt begging for mercy. When I stared at him, I didn't hide my defiance nor my disgust.

"Okay," Jesus said. He pointed Billy toward my bag in the trunk. "The memory stick is in the top zipper pocket."

Sick of talk and delay, Billy bent to reach into the trunk. Jesus slammed the lid down on the back of Billy's neck hard. It wasn't enough force or weight to break it, but it gave the old man enough pain to erase his brain for a few seconds.

Billy recovered with surprising strength and launched himself at Jesus. He had height and weight on Jesus so they both went down, rolling over each other in the dust.

Bruder watched the wrestling match, his stony expression for once replaced with surprise.

Someone else's moment of indecision is the time to move. I went at Bruder alone.

I had never fought such a large man. I had about a one in five chance of surviving the next few seconds.

Mom's first rule of fighting: Deal with the weapon before you deal with the man. I was much shorter than Bruder so I used that and came up under his extended fist. I seized Bruder's gun hand in both of mine.

Mom's second rule: The gun will go boom the moment you grab for it, so be out of the way when it goes off.

Bruder's gun boomed harmlessly in the air as I shifted my grip. As long as my hand stayed wrapped around the cylinder, the revolver couldn't blow out the back of my skull. My chances of surviving went up to two in five, for as long as I could hold on.

Wrestling with the gun left Bruder with a free hand to hit me in the face. I didn't see those jabs coming. He was younger and faster than old Billy and I was far too preoccupied with the pistol to roll with Bruder's punches. My head rocked back and I saw stars.

Mom's third rule: Don't back down. "That's why I have never lost a fight with your father," she told me. "The argument's never over until *I* say it's over and it's not over until he agrees I'm right."

Fourth rule: Fighting hurts. "If you must fight, win. You can win any fight as long as you are ready to put up with more pain than your enemy, but you gotta end it quickly."

My parents had accidentally sent me to a pervert to learn about guns. The following Saturday night, Mom took me to my first Krav Maga class. She stayed to watch every move. "I know your friends are into yoga," she said, "but your friends aren't as pretty as you."

"Mom!"

"You need to know, life is hard. Being bendy and paying some asshole in a ponytail and short shorts to tell you you're breathing wrong? Nah. That isn't going to save your life. Life isn't yoga class. Someday, everybody gets tested. I want to make sure you pass."

Mom attended every one of my martial arts classes for years. She watched in silence from the sidelines, never looked at her phone or brought a book. Mom was so vigilant because she wasn't the type to forgive or forget, not after what happened with Carmine. "Some people might call it a grudge. I call it learning," she said.

My instructors thought she was an overprotective mother watching her baby learn takedowns, punches and kicks. She wasn't worried about me getting punched in the face at the Y. She was there to watch them.

Fifth rule: Give your opponent pain before you attempt a grappling maneuver.

I stomped on Bruder's instep. He barely flinched. If Bruder thought to step back and rip his trapped weapon away from me, my chances of survival would have slipped down to zero in seconds. The big man was already pulling me off balance.

My next kick went to the inside of his knee. Bruder didn't flinch. Since I was off balance, the force of the blow wasn't what it needed to be. He sunk a little from the pain, but kept trying to pull the revolver back instead of giving it one good yank.

My grip on the pistol was slipping and I was out of helpful rules from my mother.

I pushed hard, closing the distance. I wasn't close enough to headbutt him, but I was close enough to scream in his ear. I did that, as high and as screechy a war cry as I could manage.

It was a good gamble and the best way to use what I'd thought was my last breath. Bruder pulled his head back and turned from my sonic assault as my left knee caught him square in the groin. He bent from the pain, eyes wide.

The details of one of my martial arts lessons came back to me. The most straightforward grappling maneuver is simple physics: No matter how much bigger and stronger the opponent, my whole hand is stronger than any two of his fingers. I bend the fourth and fifth fingers of his gun hand back. Bruder was driven to his knees.

I got the muzzle to his forehead. The cylinder was free to turn and the big thug's index finger was bent back, trapped by the trigger guard. Bruder froze at the realization that he was had.

My chances of surviving the fight with Bruder had shot up to five out of five. His chances? About the same as mine a few seconds before. It's only then that I wonder what happened to Jesus and Billy. I didn't dare glance back to look for him.

"Jesus?" I called.

"Still here."

In a second, Jesus came up beside me. He held a pistol I hadn't seen before so I assumed it belonged to Billy.

"You okay?" Jesus looked concerned as he pointed the weapon at my prisoner's head. He must have looked to Jesus like he was about to make a move because he cuffed Bruder's left ear and told him. "Stop, man. Don't do anything stupid. She's got you and I've got you locked."

"Where were you?" I ask. "Stop somewhere for lunch?"

"Billy tried to stab me to death."

"He dead?"

"Napping. I choked him out."

"Eventually! What do you want to do? We can put Billy in the trunk and drive it into the ocean. Or maybe feed him to the sharks?"

With Jesus covering Bruder I stepped back, still breathing hard. I liked the weight of Bruder's gat in my hand. I'd held a lot of pistols in my life but I'd never taken one away from a big brute. Victory is sweet. "What do we do now?"

I looked to the seaplane at the end of the pier. "I don't suppose you know how to fly a plane to Uruguay?"

Jesus shook his head. "Not in my skill set."

I considered this for a moment. "Bruder is wanted, right?" I suggest. "Between him and the memory stick, we could bargain with the FBI, maybe. Turn State's witness and — "

Bruder growled as he rose up from his knees.

"Bruder! Behave!" Jesus ordered.

I didn't wait. I pulled the trigger and Bruder fell dead in the dirt from a shot to the head. The report echoed through the trees and everything seemed extra quiet for a moment, as if the world suddenly began to listen intently, counting sins and judging harshly.

There was a lot of blood. I'd shot people in the head before but this death seemed extra stupid. What kind of arrogance made him think he'd survive dealing with two guns? I guessed Bruder didn't get punched in the face enough as a kid. His strength and intimidation was unearned. Huge big bullies don't learn humility the way the rest of us do. That or, like Bruder, they learn too late.

I shook and only then did I realize my face hurt. A lot. I couldn't skate on adrenaline forever. When that wore off, I'd need a lot of Advil.

Jesus pulled me into his arms and held me tight.

"Damn, Jesus."

"You did good, Lily."

"I know but why does it have to be this hard? Why couldn't they just leave us alone? And what do we do now? A few more bloody deaths and this could become a habit. I don't want to end up in court. The news would give me a stupid nickname, like Killy Lily. That would suck."

"Billy's still alive. We could find some use for him."

"Like what?" I asked.

"Use him for information, first. After that, I'm not sure. Not yet. I'm making this up as I go along."

"Like always," I said.

At that moment, Billy woke up and started to pull himself to his feet. Emerging from behind the woody wagon, his nose was broken and bleeding profusely. Billy seemed groggy, as if he wasn't entirely sure where he was. He patted his pockets, searching for a smoke, his wallet or a weapon. I'm not sure what.

Jesus and I point our pistols at him and, by the look on his face, I guessed his head began to clear.

"Well, shit," Billy said.

Then he looked down and I followed his gaze. A knife was sticking out of his side. Billy touched it gingerly and winced.

"Don't pull it out," Jesus ordered. "It will do as much damage coming out as it did going in."

Billy nodded and swayed and slowly raised his hands. "I got a thick wad of cash. Will that buy me a ride to the hospital?"

"It might have, but you hit Lily," Jesus said. "I didn't care for that. Where's the money?"

"Fuck you."

"Rude. Don't make me come over there and jiggle that blade around," I said.

"It's in a rubber band rolled up under my spare tire," he said.

"Good boy!" I said. "Now sit or I'll make you play dead."

"We should probably figure something out," Jesus said. "If we stuff him in the trunk, he's going to bleed all over our luggage."

"I knew I should have got the hard case Samsonite," I said. "It wipes clean easier. That's what I want. To wipe everything clean … to erase everything,"

"We're not talking about luggage anymore, are we?" Jesus asked.

"We are not."

B illy was ready to give us all the information we asked for. In fact, he wouldn't shut up. A knife in the gut does change one's perspective. We got what we needed out of him, but mostly it was Billy's cell phone that proved most useful. That gave us ideas about how to stir up some shit between the Family and the Machine.

Jesus sat Billy up in the trunk. The three of us watched the inland waterway beyond the seaplane we couldn't use. I thought about trying to get Billy to fly us, but he was so pale, it was obvious he'd lost too much blood and was too far gone. He could take off, but he could never land us safely which, I suppose, is the most important part.

Five pelicans zoomed just above the water searching for fish. They flew in formation like fighter aircraft. At intervals, they dove to retrieve fish. In the day's dying light, the pink sunset burned to orange and the pelicans turned into silhouettes of pterodactyls on patrol. It was such a beautiful sky, it looked fake.

As Billy sat in the trunk between us, he whimpered occasionally but got quieter and quieter. I sat on the edge of one fender and Jesus sat on the other, both of us drinking Cokes we found in Bruder's car. It had been parked between a couple of dilapidated buildings.

"Bruder won't be in the sequel," Jesus said. "Stupid. He'd be alive if he'd listened to reason."

"We almost made it out," I said.

"Almost didn't, too."

"You never thought we were going to make it, did you? You don't look surprised."

"I'm just used to things not working out as planned, that's all."

"Everything is supposed to work the way it's supposed to work."

"Doesn't," he replied.

"Never?"

"You ever tried to do anything as simple as put a piece of IKEA bedroom furniture together in less than two hours? That seems reasonable, too."

"Hm."

"You know I love my caper movies," Jesus said. "George Clooney pulling a heist and all that shit is awesome. But everything that's so slick on screen takes eight hours and five trips to the hardware store in real life."

"Murphy's Law," I said. "Anything that could go wrong — "

"Surely screws you over," Jesus finished.

Billy surprised us by still being alive as darkness slowly crept in. "For a guy by the name of Jesus, you don't have much faith."

Jesus took a long swig of his soda and looked back at Bruder lying in the grass behind the car. I hoped we'd leave before a colony of ants found the big man and started to go to work.

"I have lots of faith," Jesus said finally. "I'm sure that whatever can go wrong, will. I think God's out to get us and when things go right, that's a moment of divine oversight."

"Grim," I said.

"Think I'm wrong?"

"I didn't think God cares enough to be out to get us. Mostly, we screw ourselves over. We don't need God's help to do that."

Billy looked at me thoughtfully. He looked like he was about to say something but then he just stared. It took me a few moments to be sure that he was dead. I leaned in and checked for a pulse. Finding none, I looked over at Jesus and shook my head.

Jesus shrugged and we went back to watching pelicans weave and wheel in the dying light. They soon gave up for the day and disappeared to wherever it is pelicans go when night falls.

I kept glancing over at Billy as if he'd take another breath, holding his last breath for a couple of minutes. "Guy wanted to be a manager of his department all his life and, within a day of achieving his dream, *pfft!*"

"He had the wrong dream," Jesus said.

We stayed quiet, a dead man between us.

"First guy you killed in a while, isn't it?" I asked.

"Yep."

"You okay?"

"Like riding a bike," he said. "Righteous kill, even in a court of law. Self-defense is what it is. I put every murder I ever committed into that category."

I could tell by his tone he didn't feel good about it and told him so.

"Sometimes it feels good," he admitted, "when I'm taking out evil. If feeling good about it was my default setting, though, I'd worry about me."

"My mom says all's fair in love and war."

"Your mom's an expert at war. I'm not sure how much she really knows about love."

"She loves me," I said.

"So much she's scary, yeah."

"So you and my mom do have something in common."

After what seemed a long time, Jesus asked me what I wanted to do since Uruguay was off the table.

"I want to go home," I said.

"To clean house?" Jesus asked.

"They won't let me run so it's time to gun."

"You want me to drive?"

"Jesus take the wheel."

We decided to take Bruder's car. At a mall somewhere, we'd find a car of the same make and model and switch license plates.

The way north was a quiet ride. We stuck to secondary roads to stay off the radar. I swallowed a few painkillers for my injuries and dumped greasy fast food on top of the pills. My stomach was upset from mixing painkillers so Jesus did most of the driving. To avoid the radio, he told me the good things he remembered from his travels. Mostly, he talked about Hollywood and the celebrities he saw. There was also an overly long discourse on the philosophy behind *The Big Lebowski*. Again.

In Kentucky, we argued about whether we should like or dislike Tom Cruise movies because of the whole Scientology thing. No conclusion was reached and that lead to a larger discussion. Neither of us wanted to watch anything by Bill Cosby or Roman Polanski again, but Jesus wanted to give Woody Allen a pass because he ended up marrying the girl he knew from childhood. "*Crimes and Misdemeanors* was too good not to forgive," he said.

"I don't care how much time has passed, Woody Allen is a creep for what he did."

"His wife seems okay with forgiveness, so shouldn't we be?"

Sensing we'd never agree, I switched topics to the best meals we ever ate. I told him it was the Peking duck I had in Vancouver that melted in my mouth. He told me I was his best meal. It was nice to hear but I knew his heart wasn't in it. He was just making conversation, keeping my spirits up. His heart had been set on Uruguay. It wasn't lust or love that had him driving me back toward the Machine's gears and teeth. It was loyalty. His greatest desire was to leave the life. Still, Jesus stuck with me.

We could have gone to the FBI with the memory stick but with our histories, I doubted we'd get a good deal. Besides, Mom would never approve of going to the cops. Fighting the mob was not good but being a rat was the worst. Cops were for normal people and I couldn't claim to be among their number, not after all that had happened. I'd been fooling myself with the nice, shiny dream of getting away and never paying a price for freedom.

I could have told Jesus to go his own way and leave New York to me. I owed him. I told myself it was okay, that he'd never abandon me, anyway. The future we'd hoped for was dead but he would have stood by my side because of all our history. I had chances to drive off without him. I could have left him at a gas station and dealt with the Machine on my own but that was not a solid strategic move. I needed Jesus so I didn't give him an out.

We didn't even talk much about going back to the Bronx. That's where our story — Jesus' and mine — began. It was only fitting that it should end there.

W e took our time coming home to New York, putting off the inevitable. Financed by the thick roll of cash we'd found under Billy's spare tire, we stayed at little B&Bs all the way home. On the fifth day since we took on Billy and Bruder, we drove into the Bronx and left the car unlocked in a bad neighborhood.

Once we were on the street, I felt lighter. "I am so glad to be rid of that car. It felt like we were driving around with a target on our backs."

"If we weren't then," Jesus said, "we are now."

"Shall we drop in on our old buddy Denny? See how he's doing?"

"We need heavier weapons first. No offense to your *abuela*, but if you're determined to go to war, one little Walther won't do."

"Got another handyman in mind?"

"Not exactly a handyman in the usual sense, but I do know where the Machine's armorer used to live. I don't know if he still lives there, but we need to find him. I don't want to buy cheap stuff off the street that isn't tested. He's the Machine's guy. He'll have everything we need and more."

My cheeks flushed. I could feel the heat. I felt like that embarrassed little girl who went back to get her purse and ended up shooting Carmine's index fingers off.

"Something wrong?"

"I don't think so."

"Really?"

"Nothing. It's just that I knew the Machine's gun guy when I was a kid. Not a good man."

"Oh?"

"It was before your time. Think Woody Allen, but much worse."

"Give Woody a break."

"Okay, think Cosby, then."

I had never told Jesus about what Carmine did or what I did to him. Besides, my father had killed the old pervert. If I'd known all that Jesus had gone through when he was a kid, I might have opened up about it.

"Jesus?"

"Yeah?"

"You ever see those maps of where all the sex offenders are?"

"No."

"Well, they're like…everywhere. Neighborhood by neighborhood, you look for red dots and there's more of those sickos than there are coffee shops."

"Hey, you don't have to tell me."

"The Machine's old gun guy was one of those guys."

Jesus looked at me as we crossed Third Avenue. "Bet that didn't go over well with the Machine. All the made guys I knew were very pro-death penalty, and that was just for anybody looking at them the wrong way."

"Dad took care of him." I was proud of that. I hadn't always felt proud of my father. We argued often. Mom wanted me to be ready to be a warrior princess. Dad was the overprotective one, always wanting me to stay a princess. Getting rid of Carmine the way they did was one of those gestures that told me my parents loved me.

I loved how, afterward, Mom took me to Krav Maga practice four times a week. She never complained about the time or expense and, as I progressed, she was proud of how I could handle myself. I felt her pride and, the better at fighting I got, the more I felt like a woman instead of a helpless girl. I never thought of my mother as the sort of woman who could ever be vulnerable. She was strong and, the more independent and strong I got, the more I was like her.

I loved how my father killed Carmine to protect me. A bad man had been erased from Earth. True to my mother's word, Carmine Malgor's name was never again spoken in our house. It was as if Carbine Carmine Malgor had never existed. No cops. No fuss. No debate. It was one of those things that made me think there was something sure in the world.

Then, when Jesus knocked on a rusted metal door in an old apartment building in Mott Haven, Uncle fucking Carbine Carmine fucking Malgor fucking opened the fucking door.

It was as if gravity was suddenly turned off. The crab sandwich I had for lunch started to come back up and I almost choked on it.

Malgor didn't wait for either of us to say anything. He raised a huge carving knife and brought it down toward my face.

esus grabbed Carmine's knife arm at the wrist and elbow, the point of the blade was just a few inches from the spot between my eyes. I swallowed that crab on sourdough back down. It didn't taste as good this time. I had shit to do. Namely: Jam a thumb in Carmine's eye. He dropped the knife and it clattered to the yellowed linoleum. He clutched his left eye and screamed as he hit the floor.

"Nice reflexes, Jesus," I said.

"Thanks. The trick is expecting trouble."

As Carmine clamped a palm over his ruined eye and shouted obscenities at me. That was rude but I suppose that was to be expected. I also noted with satisfaction that he had one thumb and three fingers on each hand. At least when I took his index fingers, my vengeance stuck.

We pushed our way into the apartment and Jesus kicked Carmine in the side to stop the screaming. His technique is surprisingly effective. Maybe it was the Italian shoes that made him pause to gasp at the sharp pain in his ribs. Those expensive shoes were very pointy.

I stuck my Walther in Carmine's crotch. That maneuver also

quieted him and gave him focus. Carmine gave me his complete attention, in fact. "Hello, Lily."

"So ... you two know each other?" Jesus asked.

My father was supposed to have killed Carmine. I'd understood I was supposed to keep my mouth shut and so I had. "Jesus, I have something to tell you. Years ago, this is the piece of shit who tried to rape me."

Jesus stared at the man at his feet. I could tell from his face, this was a revelation. "I wish you'd told me earlier. I've known Carmine since Denny pulled me into the Machine." A storm built behind Jesus' eyes.

"I didn't tell you because — "

"Doesn't matter," Jesus said. "You've told me now." He gave Carmine another vicious kick from the blind side, hitting the same spot in the ribs. If Carmine didn't already have a cracked rib, he probably did then.

"You didn't tell me about your history, either," I said.

"I know. I'm sorry about that, too. If this kind of thing wasn't so...I dunno."

"Packed with shame?" I asked.

"It's not your fault," Jesus said. "Victims often blame themselves. I did for a while but — "

"Oh, I don't blame myself," I said. "I blame this fuck. That and I'm pissed off at my dad. He told me he took care of Carmine already."

Jesus crouched in front of Carmine and rolled him over onto his back. The pervert was too fragile to resist. He rolled over onto his back as if he was a big friendly dog hoping for a belly scratch.

"How about that, Carmine? Lily wants to know how it is you're still alive?"

"Bitch took my trigger fingers already."

Jesus looked up at me and I think that was newfound respect in his eyes. "You took his index fingers? That was you? I heard that part of the story but — "

"Of course, it was me. Who did you think did it?"

"Never heard directly. There was speculation. Carmine has been telling people for years it was Yakuza who took his pointers because of a bad poker bet."

I rolled my eyes. "Yakuza? Those guys cut off their *own* fingers when they fuck up. They don't do it to other people. They just kill. That was what Dad was supposed to do!"

Jesus shrugged. "Never said I believed the stories. Big Denny believed Carmine, though. I thought there was probably a simpler explanation, careless with car doors, maybe."

"You really didn't know it was me?"

Jesus shook his head. He looked too surprised to lie. He poked Carmine on the shoulder gently. Then he slapped him across the face. "How about it, horndog? Anything to contribute? Why aren't you dead?"

Carmine seemed to gather his energy to reply. Jesus slapped him again, harder. I knew why. If it takes someone too long to answer, it's because they're making shit up.

"It was business! I have connections!" Carmine bawled. "I'm valuable! To your father and the Machine, I was an earner so he let me live. If it makes you feel any better, your Dad beat the shit out of me. He beat the shit out of me really bad. One of my kidneys hardly works no more thanks to him! And I had to stay away! It was like I was a ghost to everyone and everything. Guys I knew for years wouldn't even pick up the phone!"

"Not quite enough of a ghost," I said.

Jesus looked up at me. "Does it make you feel any better?"

"My father's dead," I said. "I-I...I thought he was a man who did what he said he was going to do."

"I had to move from my home and set up in this shit kennel!"

Carmine's voice climbed to a higher, tremulous register. He sounded like a scared little girl, threatened and humiliated.

"The Machine took my guns and your father made me work for next to nothing. He held what I did over my head for the rest of his life. When I go to the market, I still can't go east because there's a school that way. I gotta go to a bodega five blocks the other direction! Your dad's dead but Denny still has guys check up on me. I got neighbors who get paid to make sure I stay inside and behave. This place? This place is my prison."

Jesus watched my face. "Carmine is sad for himself but he doesn't strike me as very contrite. What do you think, Lily?"

"Let's just get what we came for." I couldn't wait to get out of there, find a hotel and have a long hot shower.

Jesus grabbed Carmine by the collar and yanked him to his feet. "You're right about one thing, Carmine, this place is a shit kennel. You're in luck — "

"She blinded me!"

"Only in one eye."

"It *hurts!*"

"Uh-huh. I think it's supposed to. We're in a shopping mood right now. Let's see your hardware."

Carmine made no more complaints. Still holding his ruined eye with one hand, he led us into a back bedroom. It smelled like cat piss and burnt cabbage. The apartment was small, but a rough hole in the wall behind a dresser opened to the next apartment. It was filled with nothing but sofas. Apparently, Jesus had been here before. He pulled the mattress out of a hide-a-bed. Carmine's arsenal sat hidden beneath the couch cushions.

It was an impressive array: Tech 9s, sniper rifles, AR-15s, body armor and a lot of ammo. As hiding spots go, it wasn't very impressive. However, living under the protection of the Spanish mob, no locals would dare come in to steal his shit. No one but us.

When I tossed another couch cushion aside, I stepped back as if I'd been pushed in the chest. A case of grenades — US Army issue — sat in a box, ready and waiting.

"What the fuck do you need grenades for, Carmine?" I ask. "The lines too long at Costco?"

"The race war didn't come as quick as I expected. Still — "

"Why grenades?"

"They aren't for using, you stupid bitch," Carmine said. "They're for selling."

"Who do you sell grenades to?" Jesus asks.

"Anybody with money."

"Anybody?"

"Told you," Carmine said. "I'm valuable. I know the people who can bring the heavier ordnance in and I know buyers. Still never managed to buy my way back into the Machine's good graces, even after your father and the captains got themselves killed off."

Jesus took a long breath. "I've seen enough. That's the hardware. Show me your software, Carmine."

"My what?"

"Your computer."

Carmine shrugged and led us back into the first apartment. He pointed to a desktop with a tiny screen.

While I covered Carmine with the Walther, Jesus looked through some files. He clicked and clicked and kept on clicking. I didn't know what he was looking for, but it took him a long time.

Finally, Jesus looked up. "Where's the stuff you don't want me to find, Carmine?"

"What do you mean?"

"You know what I mean."

Carmine shook his head and winced. Moving his head too much made his ruined eye hurt more.

"Guys like you don't get cured, Carmine," I said.

"Guys like me?"

"Guys who go after kids."

"I'm not into that, not anymore. Your dad set me straight."

Jesus got up in Carmine's face, his voice low and threatening. "Old Pete Vasquez's influence reaches out to you from beyond the grave, does it? Is that what you're telling me? Butter wouldn't melt in your mouth? You learned your lesson and all is right with the world?"

"Sure," Carmine said. "That's what I'm telling you. Who said different?"

Jesus looked under the bed. Carmine said nothing. Then Jesus took two quick strides and opened a closet door wide.

"Get out of that. That's my personal property!"
That told us all we needed to know.

Jesus pulled a chain hanging from a lightbulb and peered at some shelves behind a few clothes hanging from wire hangers. It didn't take Jesus long to toss the closet.

The pornography came out first as he threw magazines on the floor at Carmine's feet. Evidently, Carmine still preferred young teenagers. Jesus pulled out a laptop next. Carmine looked down the mouth of my Walther with his one good eye and began to cry. "Can I get a Tylenol? Or something stronger?"

"No," I said.

"Where's your sense of mercy, Lily?"

"I still have flashbacks sometimes, you know. Remember how you came after me? I do. I can close my eyes and see it all clearly as if it's happening again. It is a sickness, *Uncle* Carmine," I told him, "but you had options. You kept your hands off me for a year. Why couldn't you leave me alone? I trusted you. Afterward, I could hardly trust anyone."

"You want an honest answer?" Carmine asked.

"If you can."

"The real answer is I came at you when I did because I wanted to get to you before you got any older."

Jesus cut him off. "That's not helping you, Carmine. How many burner phones you got?"

"Three."

"I need them all, plus your passwords."

"If I cooperate, you promise not to kill me?"

"Absolutely," he replied. "We're on a fact-finding mission tonight. I swear I won't kill you. You have my word. Now stop fucking around because we aren't fucking around."

Carmine gave us what we needed and Jesus checked to make sure he told the truth. When he was certain we had all the data we could use, he put a hand under Carmine's chin, forcing the older man to look him in the eye. "There are disturbing pictures on your laptop."

Carmine tried to look away but Jesus wouldn't let the cyclops take the easy out.

"There's a camera in the closet, Carmine."

"Yeah."

"You didn't reform your ways at all, did you?" Jesus reminded me of my father then, except it turned out my father chose business over protecting his own daughter. Pete Vasquez often railed against men who didn't do what they said they would do. Now I understood where his anger came from. He was one of those men, after all. I wondered briefly if my mother knew Carmine was still alive but that was inconceivable.

"If I looked, I'd find pictures of kids on that camera, right?"

"Maybe a few."

"Local girls, from the neighborhood? Little girls?"

Carmine said nothing.

"Lily's right," Jesus said. "It is a sickness. I knew a guy once who felt your urges. The difference was, he went out into the woods and stayed away from children. He saw something in himself that he knew was unacceptable and he isolated himself from temptation —
"

"I tried that."

"Yeah? You tried that or Pete tried to limit you? The neighbors paid to watch you maybe aren't doing such a good job, huh? Maybe they got lax over the years or maybe you're paying them off, too. How about it, Carmine? Yes? No? Maybe so?"

"Could be, a little. I try to keep it under control. I thought as I got older — "

"That's a yes, Carmine." Jesus used to be a cop. I never thought about it until now, but when Jesus was in cop mode, he didn't sound any different from my dad when he would squeeze someone to get the truth. Dad's job was dealing with deadbeats. The tone and tactics matched up pretty well.

As Pete Vasquez's daughter, it wasn't even a good idea to eat cookies without permission in my house. In my father's eyes, every case was a federal case, even if the issue was how many chocolate chip cookies my mother and I left for him. Dad's self-righteousness made his failure to erase Carmine all the more egregious.

"I need help," the pervert whined.

Jesus stared at him a moment longer. "You did need help. It's too bad you didn't act on the urge to seek help — "

"But it's been years and you're the same!" I shouted.

Without turning away from Carmine, Jesus asked me to go find body armor that fit and to start putting weapons and the grenades in a big duffel bag.

"He wasn't taken care of," I told Jesus. "It's time."

"It is." Jesus strapped a knife to his forearm. It was a large flat throwing knife. "I haven't used one of these in years," he said. "It always looked cool in the movies but it's usually impractical in real life. I loved how Sean Connery took out a guy with a throwing knife in *The Rock*. After he nails the guy with the knife, he tells Nicolas Cage's character, 'You must never hesitate.'" Jesus said it again, doing his best Sean Connery impression, "*You musht nevah heshitate.*"

Jesus tested the edge of the blade with his thumb gingerly. "You have to feel the knife for sharpness, feel for the tiny separation of the fibers of your skin. Not enough to draw blood, just enough to feel the blade doing its work. Shame, this blade is very dull."

"Don't," Carmine whispered.

"You went after kids," Jesus said, "and you tried to stick a big knife in the middle of Lily's face as soon as you saw her. That's enough, Carmine. Haven't you had enough?"

When Jesus promised he wouldn't kill him, I'd assumed he'd leave the deed to me. Instead, Jesus shoved the point of the blade through the side of Carmine's throat in a flash. The blood ran fast, pumping out in gouts of blood that sprayed the wall.

"Don't die surprised. When I said I wasn't going to kill you, I wasn't being completely honest. But you knew that, didn't you? I was trapped in a basement by monsters like you," Jesus said. "Trapped for years. Justice delayed is justice denied, so this is the best I can do. Connery was right. You must never hesitate."

Carmine sank to the floor and, as the light died in his remaining eye, it occurred to me that he lived a much longer life than he should have expected. He died never seeing the race war he was so sure would come. He never got to shoot people at random for fun as he wandered neighborhood streets.

My father didn't only betray me when he chose business over family. Carmine had caused a lot of damage to many young girls and that was on Dad and Vincent Lima, too.

"First, Billy, now, Carmine," I said.

"When they're especially evil, it's easy peasy lemon squeezy," Jesus replied.

"Starting to get back into the killing thing, huh?"

Jesus bent to wipe the blood from his blade on Carmine's pants. "Starting to warm up, picking up the pace, yeah. Wait till you see what happens next."

A feeling of calm slipped over me, as if I'd suddenly stepped out of a windstorm and found a haven. I thought of how so many of my mother's stories ended with, "And we didn't have to deal with that deserving fool again."

Carmine was a deserving fool. Maybe the world was no wiser but with his death we all had a little less to fear.

W e got Big Denny De Molina's number from Carmine's phone. Jesus put him on speaker so we could both listen to the Machine's godfather scream at us.

Jesus didn't start with hello. His first words to Denny were, "Already back from Florida?"

"Lawyers, man. We worked things out."

"Really?"

"Enough about me. I'm not very happy with you, Jesus. I'd go so far as to say I'm displeased. You really jacked me up."

"Hi, Denny!" I put in. "It's Lily."

"Still alive, huh, princess? I tried to warn Jesus not to succumb to your fuckin' charms."

"Actually, it was me who gave in to his charming fucking."

"Hilarious as always."

"You went down to Florida personally," Jesus said.

"And we all know you don't like to get out of bed for anything but breakfast, lunch and dinner," I added.

Jesus gave me a look that told me to stop helping. "Look, this is easy, Denny. You want the memory stick. We need to meet."

"Sure. Come by the shop on 111th. You know the place. We'll talk."

"The place where we reenacted that scene from *Godfather* for real? With the gun behind the toilet tank, killing Sollozzo and McCluskey?"

"Heh. Yeah — "

"No thanks. I don't need that kind of drama. You think I lost some IQ points since we talked last?"

"Around Lily Vasquez, yes, I think you lose IQ, that's for sure. When she's around, not all the blood gets to your brain."

"Nice."

"Listen to me, Jesus. You owe me. I saved your ass in L.A. Lily left you in New York — "

"You tried to kill me in New York, Denny."

"All things being equal, it's a contest to see who betrayed who most, brother. I sent you on a mission — "

"You knew I'd find Lily but you must have known I wouldn't kill her."

"Did I trust you to follow through? No."

"That's why you sent more soldiers out to follow me or find her. That led to a bloodbath in Camberley. An innocent girl died in London."

"Huh. A lot of the time I manage to make a lot of money on the side bets. Guess that didn't work out this time."

"A lot of people died who didn't have to, Denny."

"You kill 'em all?"

"In England? No, that was Lily."

"*Jeezus!* Our little girl's all grown up!" Denny said. "What's the new deal you want now?"

"I've got something valuable to trade," I said.

"The information Panama Bob took, sure," Denny replied. "It took us more than a year to figure it out after you took off. Bob was planning to go to the feds and bury us. He skimmed too much off the top and lost his nerve. He was right to be scared. You should be afraid, too, Lily."

"How'd you find out exactly?" I asked.

"His widow came forward, looking for more money. She blatted the truth."

"That explains a lot," I said. "Panama Bob's widow went to the Family looking for money, too. Miguel told us."

"Playin' us at both ends," Denny said. "*Shit.* There's somebody else's hash I'm going to have to settle before this is over."

"So let's put it all to rest," Jesus said. "When you've got the memory stick, you get freedom. No trouble from us or the feds. Lily and I get out clean. How about it? How about we show each other mercy and go our separate ways? No tricks, no drama — "

"And don't come heavy," Denny interrupted. "I know the schtick."

"So when and where?"

"The barn," Jesus said.

Denny laughed. "The usual time?"

"Glad you remember."

"When I'm not thinking of the times we tried to kill each other, I remember the other times, sure." Then Denny hung up.

"Uh, where and when is the meet?" I asked.

"It's an inside joke. You know the movie, *Midnight in the Garden of Good and Evil?* Kevin Spacey long before Spacey's fall? John Cusack?"

"Vaguely."

"That's when and where we're meeting him: Midnight in the Garden of Good and Evil. Getting the meeting was easy. Surviving will be the test."

After a trip to a hardware store where we bought a saw, Jesus and I arrived very early to set up. I was surprised to find it was a vast abandoned arena.

"Before the bottom fell out of the economy in 2008, they used to hold horse contests here."

"Dressage and rodeos, you mean?" I said.

"Yeah," he said. "Horse contests, rich people games."

"How do you know this place?" I asked.

"It's a big patch of soft dirt in the Bronx that's covered by a roof.

Lots of privacy after hours, even when this place was in operation." Jesus told me this as if he'd explained everything.

I quirked an eyebrow at him and he just stared back, waiting for me to work through it. Then I got it. "Soft dirt in the middle of the Bronx. Oh, I get it. How many bodies are buried here, Jesus?"

"More than one, less than a bunch. We had to use a backhoe and a grader. It was the closest I came to getting a job in construction when I came back to New York."

"You never told me much about what you did for the Machine."

"Now you know why. I was never proud of it. I was just trying to survive. Looking back, I guess we should have told each other more about the past."

"I did ask once or twice," I said.

"Yeah, but I thought you just wanted to know about old girl-friends."

"You really never knew about Carmine Malgor? I always worried that the guys would talk, you know, rumors and gossip. I didn't want to hang out with guys in the Machine because I was afraid they'd look at me differently. I got over that with you but I always wondered a little."

"Some things, we don't talk about, even when we kidded around. Given that your father didn't kill Carmine, you can see why no one who knew anything about it would breathe a word."

"Dad would have been embarrassed. Vincent should have let Dad kill Carmine."

"Vincent Lima was a tough boss," Jesus said. "And very practical."

"I'm just glad nobody knew," I said.

"Not even Denny said anything," Jesus assured me, "and he was just about the worst gossip in the Machine. Not as bad as Panama Bob, of course, but pretty bad."

"My father didn't want his failure getting back to me."

"Pete probably didn't want your mother to find out he didn't off Carmine."

"Yeah, she'd have killed them both. Does it ever seem to you that everybody worries about everything but when the hammer falls, we find out we were always worried about the wrong things?"

"Frequently," he agreed.

Jesus' loyalty made my father's lack of action all the more galling. I pushed that thought away and got to work to make sure everything was set for our meeting with Denny.

A high catwalk ringed the inside of the roof and, with the lamps hanging below us, we were safe among shadows. Pigeons nested among the struts that supported the vast roof. This place might have been the quietest spot in all of the Bronx. From high up, Jesus and I had a commanding view of the entire building.

"Denny will come heavy," Jesus said. "That's the only way this ends."

"So we'll come in heavy, too. Since Carmine came after me as a kid, I've always trusted guns more than I trust people."

"That explains a lot, but are you sure this is the life you want, Lily?"

"It's not what I want, but *in* is the only way *out*."

When an animal is trapped, there's nothing left but to fight. We'd been hunted too long. Tonight, we would become the hunters. A new energy shook through me and made my hands tremble. I recognized the sensation. An unquenched thirst for vengeance feels remarkably similar to guzzling a quadruple espresso.

W e each had a large jerry can full of kerosene. I suggested gasoline, but Jesus said kerosene burns longer. One large door stood at each end of the barn. I wanted to dump the kerosene over the exits as soon as we arrived. Jesus insisted we wait until we were sure Denny's goons were deep in the trap. "They'll come early to scout this place. If they see or smell the fuel, they'll rabbit."

A wooden ladder led to the roof and a series of hatches meant to cool the barn in summer. From there, we could jump to two other buildings and climb down to safety once the trap was sprung. While we waited, Jesus pulled a couple of subs out of his pack as I checked our weapons. Carmine Malgor was an asshole, but he was liberal with the gun oil and took care of his arsenal.

I decided on an Uzi and the Walther my mother gave me. I shrugged into a ballistic vest and rechecked my weapons, nervous and eager for the night to be over.

We picnicked on the roof and watched the sun sink. It wasn't like the sunset in Florida. New York's lights beat back the night so the city is never swallowed by darkness. The only darkness is in our hearts.

"You look sad. What's on your mind?" Jesus asked.

"Spain."

"I wish I was in Spain right about now, too," he said.

"I was thinking of the last time I was on a roof."

"Oh? Are you Batman? Hell of a time for you to get around to telling me, Lily."

"I spent a lot of time in Madrid but, a few times, I got out into the countryside. One night, it was sweltering. I stayed in a little town, no bigger than this block. I can't even remember the name of the village. Maybe it didn't even have a name. It was just a village beside a road, the sort of place most people pass by and the tourists only find by accident. I was sweating in my bed and couldn't sleep, but music was coming from somewhere. A beautiful guitar played softly in the distance. I went out into the hallway. The place I stayed, it was just four tiny rooms for travelers and one bathroom. The place seemed empty so I followed the music up a staircase to the roof. The owners of the place were up there with their children. The mom and dad played and the kids danced. I wish you could have been there."

"Sounds relaxed."

"It was! Just me and a couple of kids, age five and six, maybe, listening to their parents play. I started dancing with the kids and … I don't know what happened but it was like I let go of everything, you know? I started laughing along with the kids and I couldn't stop. All at once, I relaxed. I think the woman dancing with those little kids was who I was supposed to be. That's when I felt my best. I wasn't looking over my shoulder. I didn't have to think about anything else. I danced and laughed and for a little while that's all the world was. The world was good."

"I'm jealous," Jesus said. "We used to go out dancing in the old days, you and me."

"We did," I said. "If you couldn't dance, I don't think we would have got together for long. It's freeing when you only have to think about one thing and the decisions aren't life and death."

"I can't remember ever being that free," Jesus admitted.

"That night on the roof with that family, the lights went out in the village. I've never been in such complete darkness. It was a clear night. When I lay back, the stars seemed so close and so bright, it was like being in space. It was like we were floating on the vibrations of guitar strings. That was some sweet magic, man."

"And now here we are, on a roof again — "

"Getting ready to do the opposite of magic," I said. "I wish you'd come with me to Spain and I wish we could have stayed there."

"Denny's gotten to be a really big guy. The planet is too small to avoid him."

"I have to push him out of my equation. We were all friends for a long time. Are you going to be able to do what needs to be done when the time comes? You've got a long history with him. This isn't going to be like it was when you got rid of Carmine."

"*Heh.* Last month I was in a coffee shop and a couple of guys beside me had an endless discussion about whether to unfriend somebody on Facebook. They'd been friends since college but had nothing in common since. Their politics didn't jive anymore."

"So?"

"This guy looked like he was in his forties and he was still caught up in whether to delete somebody he thought was a douchebag. I wanted to tip his mocha frappuccino in his lap and tell him to be a man and end it. They didn't have anything in common anymore and that inertia was yanking his chain decades on. It was pathetic."

"And with you and Denny?"

"More than the money and the memory stick, Denny wants you dead. That's the end of the argument."

"Yeah. Still, I'm sorry to put you in this position — "

"The man I considered a brother is making me choose. That's on him, Lily. I don't want to but that doesn't mean I won't. We have to do lots of things we don't want to do."

"Thanks for choosing me, Jesus."

When he looked at me, I saw love in his eyes. When the connection is that strong, is love a choice? I don't think so. Love is something that happens to you, like a disease.

"There are four grenades in the bag," Jesus said. "If the play goes sideways — "

"Pull the pin, hug it to my heart and see what happens next," I said. "I know."

Jesus looked through the duffel and drew out an Uzi to match mine. "They aren't guitars but I know their music. These instruments can make a lot of people float away."

The scout arrived at the barn's east door, seventy feet below me. He had a neckbeard, maybe trying to hide his extra chins. I didn't recognize him from the Machine. He checked the perimeter of the arena's ring.

At one point, he looked up in my direction. It seemed he was looking directly at me. With every step, I wondered if Neckbeard could hear me breathing. He paused for a long time, maybe searching for an odd shape amid the shadows, perhaps just listening. Finally, he moved on.

When he got to the other end of the building, he appeared to be looking for a way up to the catwalk.

Good luck with that, I thought. There was only one ladder and, once we climbed it, Jesus sawed it away from the wall, pulled it up and left it on the roof. The only way to reach us was with bullets.

Satisfied he was alone, Neckbeard pulled out his phone. In rapid Spanish, he made his report. I couldn't see Jesus from where I was crouched. I wondered if passing the first test had left him more relaxed or more tense at what was to come.

A few minutes passed before a long black Caddy pulled through the east door and drove to the center of the barn. Nobody got out of the car but Neckbeard climbed in the back. The vehicle was armored. Big Denny wasn't taking any chances. We didn't have to wait long for the other player to arrive.

A blue Mercedes pulled through the west door, just as Jesus had instructed. The car slid to a stop and two men stepped out. One was obviously a bodyguard stuffed into a suit that didn't fit. He had the huge jaw of a steroid abuser and a bodybuilder's physique that cried out for yards more material and custom tailoring for that suit. He carried an AR-15, ready but not pointed anywhere dangerous yet.

I recognized the other man, middle-aged and serious. I'd met him at a party at Miguel's place once. I didn't remember his last name, but his first name was Perry. I remembered it because it seemed so unlikely that a mobbed-up guy could be named Perry. His mother probably hoped he'd become a dentist when she named him, not the head of the Family.

The driver stepped out of the Caddy, a large bald man carrying a submachine gun. He nodded at the Family's bodyguard and the big guy nodded back.

The Caddy's back door opened and Big Denny climbed out behind Neckbeard. "Evening, Perry!"

"Hey, Denny."

"Cold night," Denny observed. "It's a lot warmer in Miami. How come you aren't in Florida, watching bikinis?"

"I like New York," Perry said. "Suits my constitution. You know what they say? If you can make it here, you can make — "

"What the fuck are you *doing* here, Perry?"

"I guess the pleasantries are over. I was about to ask you the same question," Perry called back.

"Where's Jesus Diaz and Lily Vasquez?" Denny demanded. "That's who I'm supposed to be meeting."

Perry shrugged, looked around, and said nothing. "That's who I'm supposed to be meeting, too. You think they're going to try to auction off all that shit they've got about the Machine again? I was told they had useful information for me — "

"That didn't work out so well last time," Denny said. "I lost two good soldiers, a third was wounded and now I got a beef with law enforcement in Florida."

"The Family lost guys at Miguel's place, too, Denny," Perry said. "And a couple more, Billy and Bruder, are missing."

"You came a long way for nothin', Perry. This is Machine territory. I won't shit in your living room if you don't shit in mine. We've had peace for a long time. Too much ambition ruins things. I've seen it happen. I'd hate to see it happen again."

"We're thinking of expanding, looking at new territories. Maybe we can work things out. You could work for me, Denny. It doesn't have to be a hostile takeover."

"The Machine is the Machine," Denny said. "If you're here, it's because you think we're weak and vulnerable. We were weak but we've been rebuilding after the shake-up. Vincent is gone. I'm in charge. We've worked it out. We are not weak, Perry, and I don't work for nobody! People work for me!"

Jesus texted me. I didn't need to look at my phone. The vibration in my pocket was signal enough. I poured the kerosene, slowly, smoothly and as quietly as possible. I knew Jesus was doing the same.

The fireworks were about to begin.

The east door burst into flame behind the Mercedes. That was my signal. I tossed a match and flame raced down the wall. There were three issues that Jesus and I didn't count on. We discovered those variables in quick succession as the fire was lit.

Issue #1: The guys from the Family and the guys from the Machine panicked when they spotted the flames.

Issue #2: As the fire burned and spread, Jesus and I were no longer ninjas in the darkness and gloom. We were targets, lit up like Christmas trees. Both parties spotted me first and began throwing shots my way. I dove behind a post and listened to the bullets chew through the wood at my back. I was pinned down.

Issue #3: The old barn was made of wood, aged and dried to combustible perfection. Smoke rose with the heat to obscure the catwalk. The smokescreen made it harder for my enemies to target me but it was harder for me to see them, too.

The smokescreen thickened enough to provide me some cover so I could move along the catwalk so I was no longer where they thought I was. The bad news was that I'd probably die of smoke inhalation before I could eliminate the heads of the Machine and the Family.

I began to choke on smoke as the first grenade went off beside the Mercedes. That was Jesus at work.

I ran along the catwalk toward the ladder to the hatch that would take me to the roof. The smoke thinned so I got a glimpse of Perry and his big bodyguard. Perry was face down in the dirt. The bodyguard was down, too, but still dangerous, firing on Jesus' position.

I paused at the bottom of the ladder and fired on the bodyguard. He was so focused on Jesus, he didn't even look my way until the slugs ripped through him. No number of sit-ups could stop hot lead from tearing through his torso.

As soon as I started shooting, Jesus ran my way, firing on the Caddy as he moved to keep Denny and Neckbeard hiding behind cover. As I sank to the catwalk to change mags, a few rounds ripped into the wall behind me. I waited for whoever was firing to change out their ammo, then rolled to the edge of the catwalk to fire down on the men from the Machine.

Neckbeard popped up and jerked back at a bullet's impact. Jesus got him with a round to the chest. Denny stood behind the Caddy. He put one hand high in the air and screamed, "I got Jesus! I'm burning you down, brother! I'm burning the whole thing down!"

That brought us to Issue #4 and it was a bigger problem than the spreading fire or the choking smoke. Denny was not calling for the cavalry on his phone. One hand is still high in the air. With his other hand, he's pulled back his shirt.

Denny laughed. "I got you, man! I got you so good!"

I froze, narrowed my eyes and peered closer. Denny was wearing a wire.

Worse, Neckbeard wasn't dead, after all. He was only wounded. Neckbeard stared up at me and managed to shout, "FBI! Drop the weapon! I'm a federal agent! Stop!"

No wonder Denny got out of Florida so quickly. Jesus was wrong about how much fancy lawyers could do for Denny. It wasn't loopholes, lies and unlikely alibis that got Denny out of trouble in Florida. It was a deal. Denny turned rat.

Jesus ran up and shoved me toward the ladder. "They'll be coming in any second! Go!"

I hurried up the ladder to the roof while Jesus covered my retreat. Neckbeard was still throwing shots but he might as well have had a cap gun at this range. I got up and out into the midnight air.

A moment later, Jesus scrambled up behind me. "Somewhere nearby, they'll have a mobile command van," Jesus said. "They'll be setting up a perimeter. We don't have time for me to say all I want to say."

"I know."

"You know what to do," Jesus said. "Imagine I said all the right things and had all the time in the world to say them perfectly without stuttering."

He kissed me once more, quick and hard, then turned back to the hatch we'd just climbed through.

"Jesus — "

He pulled the pin on two grenades and dropped them through the hatch.

Denny screamed once more. *"Jesus! Bastardo!"*

We were friends once. I thought I didn't want to see Denny De Molina ripped apart by shrapnel. Then I thought how much he wanted me dead and I discovered something about myself: All things considered, I really did want to see that. But there was no time.

Two big, tinny bangs rang out.

When I looked back, Jesus had disappeared. Wherever he went, the FBI would be after him. He'd do what he could to lead them away. A long trail of outlaw behavior had condemned us to always being chased by the authorities. However, chaos and confusion were allies, too. As the abandoned arena lit up in flames behind me, destruction bred confusion.

Since I left New York, the FBI and the Machine had been after both of us. I saw only one way to cut that heat in half. It meant giving up all hope of ever attaining that feeling I'd once had on a roof in a village in Spain.

By the time the fire engines arrived, I was already four blocks away, melding with the crowd. I smelled a little of smoke but otherwise, I blended in. I could have been like anyone else on the street.

The tactics of my escape were simple but effective. My jacket was reversible so I went from a black to red. I dumped my weapons in a dumpster. All but one.

By the time I got out the other end of an alley, I was wearing a blonde wig. Cop cars swung into view and I turned left. It's hard to force yourself to saunter casually when you're a fugitive, but the city's streets worked with me. With all the sirens wailing and rising bedlam, crowds began to form. I became another face in the crowd, looking up, passive, watching others' dirty deeds.

After a while, I slipped away and went to a movie. The movie featured Melissa McCarthy playing a funny woman doing things no real human would do and, in the end, learning a valuable lesson about believing in herself…or some goddamn thing.

I hardly paid attention. I searched for Jesus in the darkness, but he didn't come. This was supposed to be our rendezvous point. By the time the movie was over, I was sweating, sure Jesus had been pinched or the FBI had killed him.

I found a motel in Hoboken and laid low for a day. The next night I went back to the Bronx, to the next place where I was supposed to meet Jesus. The backup rendezvous was a diner on East 164th Street. I ate slowly to give him lots of time to find his way back to me. As I sat in my booth alone, a police cruiser rolled up. Then another arrived. Two uniformed officers of the NYPD strolled in, surveyed the place, and took the booth behind me.

I strained my hearing, but the men hardly spoke at all. Another cruiser slipped into the parking lot, followed by a black car with two men in front. As the men stepped out, I was sure they were either feds or detectives.

Scared to get up, I sipped cold coffee and played a word game on my phone. I wondered if they were playing with me, waiting until I stepped outside before attempting to arrest me so there'd be fewer civilians in the line of fire.

I dared furtive glances at the newcomers' reflection in the window glass. The detectives seemed to stare at me and I wondered if my wig was on straight. I was sure I was caught right up until the moment a red Stingray slid into view. No one got out of the car but I knew who it must be.

I took a deep breath and somehow knew everything was going to work. I got up and ignored the men behind me. I left some money for the waitress on the table and strode out of the diner, head held high. With each step my confidence grew and by the time I hit the parking lot I was strutting as if I'd never experienced a moment of fear in my entire life. I didn't allow myself to cry until I slid into the passenger seat beside my mother.

She looked at me coldly. "How long have you been in town without calling?"

"Mom!"

She started the engine and pulled out. We left the cops behind us. Mom dug into her coat. "I got some flowers from my florist," she said, "but the bouquet of red roses was for you. It came with this."

She handed me a crumpled note. I already knew it was Jesus saying goodbye. He understood what I had to do. He also knew that, as much as he loved me and I loved him, we couldn't be together.

I read the note in the red glow of the next stoplight:

I guess we won't be getting the Family and the Machine to kill each other, after all. If Denny hadn't become an informant, he would have come at Perry guns blazing as soon as he got out of his Caddy.

Freedom is not just about getting away from the Machine now. The feds want me so badly, they'll even bargain with Denny. We have to split up if either of us is to have a chance at a new life.

Not to get too Shawshank on you, but I want to see that rooftop in Spain you talked about. If I can make it happen, maybe I'll see you there someday. For now, you'll have a better chance without me. If I stick with you now, I'll only bring more heat from the feds your way. I do this because I love you.

~ JD

We'd talked about Uruguay and we dreamed of escaping to French Polynesia. We had dreamed about a lot of places that didn't have extradition treaties, too. None of that mattered. Dreams are just dreams. Getting away together was like dreaming of winning the lottery: fun to think about, but extremely unlikely.

"I haven't seen you cry often, not even when you were little," Mom told me. "The little Cuban must be something special."

"Yes."

"Sorry, but you'll replace him. Meet somebody normal."

"I'm not normal."

"You're better than normal," she said. "You're not weak. Life is war and weakness is the enemy."

I liked life better when it was a dance. I didn't share that with my mother. She would have called that sappy sentimentality. Dad always said Mom was born hard. "You can try to smooth her out," he told me, "but your mama's a cold stick of butter that tears up the bread."

She had tried to make me in her image. To survive, I'd have to be even more like her. I'd have to stay away from men, too, if only to save them.

"Mom? Did you know Carmine was alive?"

"*Carmine?* Carbine Carmine? He's alive?"

"He's dead now."

"Oh. Good. Wait. Are you saying you're father didn't kill him?"

"Carmine earned for the Machine. Papa Vincent must have not given the okay to kill him and Dad was too scared to tell you the truth."

Mom gritted her teeth. "You think he was afraid of me? I don't think he was scared enough. If I'd scared him more, it wouldn't have mattered what his boss said! Damn that man."

"Carmine Malgor is dead. Vincent Lima is dead. Dad's dead. Big Denny De Molina wasn't too big to die, either."

My mother made an impatient *tsk* sound. "I'm hearing rumblings, Lily. What's left of the Machine is going to have to go to war with the Family. The head of the Family is dead. They wanted in on our territory. With Perry gone, they'll want all our blood, too. The other New York families are saying we're on our own. They sense weakness. Where's my money going to come from, then? Denny's been taking care of me!"

"Really?"

"Yeah."

"Well, that's over. The apple cart is upset."

"*I'm* upset," Mom said.

"Have you heard anything from the crew?"

"No."

"Then let's go somewhere and call everybody. I've got their numbers."

"Everybody?"

"Everybody who isn't pinched yet. God knows how much Denny told them about the organization."

"Then what?" Mom asked.

"Whatever is left of the Machine will need to get reorganized."

"Lily, if we drive all night, I could get you to an airport and you could grab a flight. Tomorrow night, you could lose yourself in L.A. or San Francisco."

"I'm back and I'm staying, Mom. I'm going to run the Machine."

"*What?*"

"Like any machine that's been broken, it can be fixed. We'll pick up the pieces, grease some wheels and make it fly again. I'm going to make it earn."

"Are you crazy?"

"Yes. That's kind of the point."

"But you could get away!"

"Not true," I said. "No matter how far I run, I'm still me. Taking over the Machine, crushing my enemies and building something where my father did not? This is my happily ever after."

She went quiet for a long time. We drove. I watched the city slide by. Soon, this will be my city again. By that, I mean I'll own it.

"There will be opposition," Mom said. "The Machine has never been run by a woman."

I reached into my purse and put my hand on my *abuela's* Walther P38K. "Men keep screwing it up. It's time a woman took the wheel. You'll help."

"Why would I do that?" she asked.

"Denny's out of the picture and you'll need money. I'll get it. To have anything, we're going to have to go for it all."

"How?"

"I'm my mother's daughter, ice in my veins."

"This is crazy."

"This is destiny. Everything that's happened until now was training for what's to come. Jesus gave me a nice vacation away from real life. Vacation time is over."

As my mother drove on to Spanish Harlem, I took the memory stick out of my bra. Jesus and I could have used the data as a bargaining chip with the feds. Denny beat us to that punch. In the end, we had to be who we are. We had to plant our feet and stop pretending.

I rolled down my window to feel the breeze on my face. I pulled off the blonde wig and threw it out the window. As we slipped through the night, the wind pulled through my hair like cool fingers. I actually managed to chuckle. I'd dreamed of a life of leisure. Sadly, I was going to have to earn it, just like anyone else.

I would never be free of the Machine. Jesus Diaz wanted out but he was always "the little Cuban," an outsider. I was born into the mob. I had to accept that I was also born *for* it.

I could not escape my history but if I embraced my parents' legacy, I might escape the Machine's wrath. I'd been a frightened girl and a little princess. Jesus treated me like a queen. It was time for me to take my rightful place as Lily Vasquez, Godmother.

It was the least I could do for the hit man who sacrificed so much and protected me even when I didn't deserve his love. I owed Jesus Diaz. He almost died for my sins.

AUTHOR'S NOTE

Thank you for reading *Resurrection*. Authors and their books live and die by reviews. If you enjoy my work, please review them and spread the happy word. A review need not be long, it helps support my work and allows me to continue writing.

Cheers!
   Robert
   P.S. You'll find links to all my books at AllThatChazz.com and more details on the next few pages.

ABOUT MY OTHER KILLER CRIME THRILLERS

I write in a variety of genres. If mystery and suspense and lots of gunplay and explosions are your reading pleasure, you may especially enjoy these killer thrillers.

The Hit Man Series

"I found myself rooting for the guy with the gun and the Armani suit." ~ Armand Rosamilia, author of *Dying Days*

The *Hit Man* books feel like *John Wick* had sex with a bunch of Coen brothers' movies.
     Fast-paced and packed with traps and twists, the wide and easy road out of town is always deadly.

Bigger Than Jesus

Jesus (it's pronounced "*Hay-soose*") Diaz is the funny hit man caught in the gears of The Machine. Jesus craves what we all want: the love of a bad woman and bags of cash. The mob wants him dead. To escape New York will take wit and grit. He's got plenty of both.

Fast-paced and packed with traps and twists, the wide and easy road out of town is always deadly.

Higher Than Jesus

Killing a guy on Christmas is bad luck. Jesus (it's pronounced "Hay-soose") Diaz is hunted by the FBI and the mob. He's also failing miserably at group therapy. From the bad streets of Chicago to the White House, secrets are revealed as badasses burn. Arms deals go sideways. Vicodin brings you up. Willow, the glamazon of your dreams, goes down. The stakes crank ever higher. You wanted a life in movies? Your life is a movie but Happily Ever After could prove elusive. Strap in for a deadly new year.

Hollywood Jesus

The unluckiest assassin meets his deadliest opponent yet. Teaming up with a rising star to break up a human trafficking ring, the action gets rough. Jesus (it's pronounced "*Hay-soose*") is tougher, or at least he'd like to think so. You're going to love Jesus!

~

The Night Man

What would you do if your father was kidnapped and your high school sweetheart's husband hurt her? What if you can't go to the cops because they're in on it?

After serving his country for years, Ernest "Easy" Jack hoped his family's reputation was forgotten. All he wants to do is train guard dogs. Unfortunately, small towns have long memories. Back from Afghanistan, the wounded warrior's new war has only begun.

Bad people will go hard on Easy. He's badder and harder.

~

Brooklyn in the Mean Time

When a wayward son returns home, uncovering the past could kill his future. Family secrets are murder.

"Sucks you in and refuses to let go! A true master of his craft!" ~ Alex Kimmell, author of *The Key to Everything*

Dangerous men want their money back and Chazz is on the run. When he discovers a side of his father he never knew, big mistakes must be buried if Chazz is to survive. Digging up the old ugly with his brother could get Chazz killed long before a drug lord's hitman shows up to collect.

Bumbling his way through '90s New York, encounter a new kind of psychological crime novel. Funny, dark and compelling, you're in for a great read on a fast ride as soon as you begin *Brooklyn in the Mean Time*.

**All book links can be found at
AllThatChazz.com.**

ABOUT THE AUTHOR

Robert Chazz Chute is a former crime journalist, speechwriter, book doctor and an award-winning writer living in Other London. He writes killer crime thrillers, suspense and epic apocalyptic science fiction. To find out more about his books and podcasts, please visit his author page at AllThatChazz.com and sign up for updates and deals.

If you really dig Robert Chazz Chute's work and crave even more crunchy interaction and sweet inky goodness, join us on the Facebook fan page here for more frequent updates and chat.

facebook.com/robert.c.chute

twitter.com/RChazzChute

instagram.com/robertchazzchute

ALSO BY ROBERT CHAZZ CHUTE

~ THE CRIME THRILLERS ~

Bigger Than Jesus, Book 1 of The Hit Man Series

Higher Than Jesus, Book 2 of the Hit Man Series

Hollywood Jesus, Book 3 of the Hit Man Series

Resurrection, A Hit Man Thriller

The Night Man

Brooklyn in the Mean Time

Sometime Soon, Somewhere Close

~

~ DYSTOPIAN & APOCALYPTIC FICTION ~

This Plague of Days, Season 1

This Plague of Days, Season 2

This Plague of Days, Season 3

This Plague of Days, Omnibus Edition

~

AFTER Life INFERNO

AFTER Life PURGATORY

AFTER Life PARADISE

AFTER Life (Box set)

~

Amid Mortal Words

~

Robot Planet, The Complete Series

~

Haunting Lessons, Book 1 of The Dimension War
Death Lessons, Book 2 of The Dimension War
Fierce Lessons, Book 3 of The Dimension War
Dream's Dark Flight, Book 4 of The Dimension War

~

~ TIME TRAVEL ~

Wallflower

~

~ COLLECTIONS ~

Murders Among Dead Trees
Self-help for Stoners
All Empires Fall

~

~ NON-FICTION ~

Do the Thing: The Last Stress-busting Book You'll Ever Need

~

All book links can be found at
AllThatChazz.com.